License to Shift

D1431581

ALSO BY KATHY LYONS

The Bear Who Loved Me

License to Shift

Book Two of Grizzlies Gone Wild

KATHY LYONS

FOREVER
YOURS

New York   Boston

Forever Yours
Hachette Book Group
1290 Avenue of the Americas
New York, NY 10104
forever-romance.com
twitter.com/foreverromance

First Edition: October 2016

Forever Yours is an imprint of Grand Central Publishing.
The Forever Yours name and logo are trademarks of Hachette Book Group, Inc.

The publisher is not responsible for websites (or their content) that are not owned by the publisher.

The Hachette Speakers Bureau provides a wide range of authors for speaking events. To find out more, go to www.hachettespeakersbureau.com or call (866) 376-6591.

ISBN 978-1-4555-4095-2 (ebook edition)
ISBN 978-1-4555-4096-9 (print on demand edition)

E3

License to Shift

Chapter 1

*F*emale.

Mark Robertson's nose twitched, and he moved to explore the scent.

Fertile.

He pursued, the spice of her as sharp as a hook.

A sound grated on his nerves and his hackles rose in irritation. The female was here and he was already thick with the drive to mount her.

Close.

He would hunt her, and she would succumb.

Part of him was uncomfortable with that predatory thought. It disliked the absolute ruthlessness with which he would claim his mate. But that voice was tiny and uninteresting. When it came to mating, there were no limits. Offspring were imperative. Taking a female urgent. He would hunt this female unto the ends of the earth.

If only the damned noise would stop.

He blocked out the sound, refocusing on the female, but she proved elusive. The scent was there, the draw undeniable, but he had to wake to find her.

Wake.

He did, though the struggle to consciousness was hard. He'd been dreaming, he realized. And someone was making a noise that pounded in his temples. The grizzly part of him wanted to obliterate the sound with his claws. The man in him barely had the wherewithal to comprehend it was the door buzzer.

He shoved to his feet, his movements lumbering and awkward. He banged into a desk and howled in rage, the sound waking him enough to open his eyes.

Home.

He was in the place bear and man coexisted in relative peace, but the sound was forcing him to leave it. That didn't bode well for whatever idiot was leaning on the buzzer. He inhaled, pulling in the scent of humming electronics, stale coffee, and fertile female.

Well, at least that part had been real. A woman stood on his doorstep, which made her easy prey.

He stumbled to the stairs, climbing angrily out of his basement den. The raw buzzer sound ate at his control, and each moment it continued made his teeth bare with fury. The man in him prayed it was the female, otherwise the grizzly would kill it. This was his most dangerous time—when bear and man fought against each other for control. It made the animal unpredictable and the man insane.

The clamor paused, giving him a split second of relief. And then it began again, the renewed racket even worse because of the brief respite.

He had no dexterity to manage the locks. The bear tried to rip the door open, but it was steel reinforced and would not budge, though God knew he tried. The frustration nearly undid the bear, but the man took control. He slammed his hand down twice trying to break the lock before he thought to twist the deadbolt. The chain was harder, requiring more focus, and his higher cortex was recruited to handle the fine manipulation. Higher cortex was controlled by the man, which forced the beast back into sullen bitterness.

This was why I layered a dozen different locks on his door, the man gloated. So it would require higher brain function to open and thereby save whatever idiot thought they could wake him. The bear remained silent, biding its time until the man managed the locks. And when the task was done, the bear attacked.

It surged to the fore, hauling on the doorknob with all its strength. It still required the man to grip the knob, but beyond that, the grizzly was in control. Worse, it was whipped into a frenzy by the buzzer and the female.

Still, the door would not open.

He roared in frustration. The grizzly wanted to rear up in fury, but since the man was already standing, this merely reinforced his upright position. And with that, a large yellow sign came into view. It was a black arrow on a yellow placard, the color so bright it hurt his eyes even in the semi-light of the front alcove.

It took the man to understand it. And it took another eon of that relentless sound for the man to establish control. That, of course, was why the newest lock and sign were there. It could only be managed by a man. The bear would destroy it, thereby trapping him indoors forever.

But he was a man still. At least enough so that he could control himself. So he beat the grizzly back, forcing it into a tight compartment of his mind where it clawed at its cage. The arrow pointed to a keyboard hung on the wall. To open the door, he had to type in six numbers and four letters. The animal had no prayer of remembering the sequence, but the man could do it, though he fumbled it twice before managing it on the third attempt.

The door unlocked with a loud *thunk* of electric magnets shutting off. Then he twisted the knob and hauled the heavy thing open.

First thing he did was slap her arm away from the buzzer. He tried to modify his strength so as to not break her arm, but the grizzly demanded violence for the assault on his ears. She gave a squeak of alarm, but it wasn't a cry of pain, so the man in him was reassured. And while she stood there, her mouth open in shock, he took the time to use all his senses, orienting himself to the world outside his den.

It was afternoon on a Michigan summer day. The sky was overcast, which was a blessing on his eyes. It also kept the air from being too hot. His home edged the Gladwin State Park, a rustic cabin that belied the expensive electronics that kept his basement a hum of activity.

But that was behind him. In front was a woman, lush and fertile.

He cared little for her coverings—crisp linen pants beneath a polyester blouse. What he focused on was the scent of her body and the flush on her cheeks. The animal in him smelled for disease and found none. He also evaluated the power in her body, the width of her hips, and the full, lush round-ness of her breasts. The grizzly pronounced her exceedingly healthy to carry young. The man liked the sight of her cleav-age and the length of her legs. Neither cared that her mouth hung open in shock, though they noted the quick tempo of her breaths.

"Uh, hello," she said. There might have been more words, but he didn't have the brain function to process sentences yet, and even if he did, her voice drowned out the sounds of the forest. He had been asleep for a while, and he needed to be alert for danger. He would brook no interference now that the fertile woman had presented herself at his door.

So when she kept speaking, he growled at her. Low and gut-tural. She snapped her mouth shut on another squeak, which he found strangely funny. He sniffed the wind, finding the usual mix of civilization and woods. Nothing of note except for this woman, whose scent mixed feminine musk with citrus. Oddly appealing.

So he turned his full attention back to her, mentally dissecting the smell—what was shampoo, deodorant, and her. He liked *her*, and he felt his organ thicken in desire.

A memory teased at his mind. Did he know this woman? He

studied her sturdy body, seeing the lush curves and wide hips, good for carrying young. If he took this woman now, she would conceive his young. He could overpower her here, rip off her coverings, and release his seed inside her within moments. It wanted it with a fierceness that alarmed the man.

So he forced himself to turn away, heading for the one thing that helped most when his control balanced on a knife's edge. It required him to turn his back on her, but he did it while he lumbered to the kitchen and the acrid scent of cold coffee.

He found it on the counter. A banged-up metal mug that waited for situations just like this. He grabbed it and swallowed the cold brew, praying it would work one more time. It would push the brain cells into life and thereby suppress the animal a little more. Then he could live for another day as a man instead of a beast.

He heard her follow him. She wasn't in the least bit quiet as her sandals slapped on the hard tile of his front hall. He heard her draw breath, probably to speak, and he whipped around to glare at her. He was not human yet. She would wait until he was. Anything else was too dangerous for her.

But when he spun around to growl at her, he was struck again by how pretty she was. Not her scent, but her features. Round face with a pert nose. Large brown eyes and curly hair pulled into a messy bun. She wore makeup, though lightly, and she'd chewed off any hint of lipstick. She had a light brown mole near her right ear just above her jaw, and he wanted to lick it to see if he could detect the change in texture with his tongue. And then there was her mouth, soft and red. She was biting her lower lip on one side. It was an endearing, human sight that made the man happy. The bear didn't care about such details. Minute shifts in expression on a human face meant nothing to it. But as long as he could see the flash of a white tooth as it tugged at her lower lip and know she was uncertain, he knew he was still a man even if he couldn't form actual words just yet.

Again that hint of knowing her teased at him, through both bear and man. She was familiar, but he hadn't the focus to isolate the memory. He needed more caffeine, but the metal mug was empty. Fortunately, he knew the next steps by heart. It was a complicated process, but that was part of the plan. The more he used his brain—even to fire up an expensive espresso machine—the better for everyone.

So he did. He turned on the machine, pulled milk from the refrigerator and honey from the cabinet. He did everything by rote, while each motion reinforced the human side of his personality. He ground the beans, measured out the espresso shots, and filled a large mug. Without conscious decision, he added chocolate and whipped cream, then drizzled the honey across the top before offering it to her.

A gift for the woman who would be his mate.

No.

The man cut off the thought, knowing that it came from the animal. This was a gift for the woman who'd risked her life by waking him. That made her stupid, not a life mate. And why the hell would she come here when she was fertile? Good God, who would be that stupid?

Every *normal* human woman would be that stupid, he answered himself. It was only the shifters who scented fertility and thought about what that broadcast to the world. Which meant this woman was fully human and completely ignorant of his kind.

He ought to throw her out of the county. Until her cycle ended, she was a temptation to every young boy in the flush of his first season. Though, if he were honest, she was in the most danger from him.

She looked perplexed as he held out the drink. He ought to be drinking it instead of giving it to her. He needed all the caffeine he could get right then. But she was his female—*a woman,* the man corrected, and not his at all. She was a woman in his home and this was as polite as he could manage. If she took it, though, that would seal her fate. The grizzly would take it as a sign of agreement to mate.

There was nothing Mark could do to stop that. Her only hope was if she left while he remained in control of himself. Which made it the man's job to get rid of her as soon as possible. For her own sake.

And all the while, he just stood there, his hand beginning to burn from the heat of the mug.

Take it, the bear urged.

Run, the man screamed. *While you still can.*

But no words formed on his mouth. And after a long, slow moment, she reached out and lifted the mug from his fingers.

Her touch was light, the brush against his skin sending bolts of desire into his hard dick. It jerked toward her, but he didn't move beyond that. And then she smiled, her expression clear enough for even the bear to understand. A wary greeting. Her face said, *Hello*. And maybe added a "thank-you" as she pulled the drink to her mouth.

He watched, mesmerized, as her lips pursed against the white cream. Her eyes drifted closed, and her throat shifted as she swallowed. Then he heard it. A soft release of sound, too quick to be a purr and yet was undeniably delight.

Oh, hell. She was appreciating his gift. His cock stood up ramrod straight, and if his muscles hadn't been locked tight, he would have reached for her. She'd accepted his gift of food, even murmured her appreciation of it. She was his now, according to the grizzly. The man wondered if she'd just signed her death warrant.

She lowered the mug and licked the cream from her lips. His breath caught, and he had to tighten his hands into fists so that he wouldn't reach for her. He had to leave before the grizzly caught him unaware. Willing or not, the bear would impregnate her because that was its number-one, absolute drive right now. *Get her with child.*

With a strangled sound, he jerked himself back to the machine. He could make his own drink and pray that the caffeine helped him keep the grizzly caged.

So long as she didn't speak. And if she touched him, she was doomed.

He began to order himself about, his mind becoming a drill sergeant to the body. Put in the coffee, slam on the machine, watch the dark liquid of sanity pour from the spout. He focused on those simple details while beside him he heard her breath catch. There'd been fear in her scent from the beginning. An acrid tang that helped keep him away from her. The man detested that scent and would do nothing to make it continue. But now he wished it would overwhelm him. Now he wanted her to be bathed in the scent because while he tried to focus on making coffee, he scented her arousal. The musk deepened, the scent akin to roasted nuts. He knew that scent. It was imprinted on his brain as clearly as a brand.

Who is she? He wanted to remember.

He finished making his latte, sweetening it only with honey before gulping it down. It seared his tongue and burned his throat, but it was better to feel pain than smell her. It was a skill he'd perfected in these last years while slowly going feral. He focused on one sensation and blocked out the rest. His throat burned, therefore he couldn't know that she was attracted to him. He couldn't be drawn in by her body's interest because all he felt was his own scorched tongue. Or so he told himself.

And then—thank God—she did something smart enough to preserve her virtue. She began to speak, her words high with nervousness and too rushed for him to process without recruiting his higher cortex.

Yes. Yes. Make me think. Make me hear. But for God's sake, don't touch me.

More words. What did they mean?

"…my father…computer…notes…have them?"

It took three tries before he could form a word. Even so it came out more like a grunt. "No," he said. Then the most important thing for her own safety. "Leave."

"...can't."

Hell.

Chapter 2

*O*MG! *OMG! OMG! OMG!*

Julie Simon was not a prude. She enjoyed a finely honed male body as much as any woman. But when said finely honed man answered his door stark naked and proceeded to look at her like she was the answer to his prayers, well, then, her libido kicked into overdrive. Especially when that look turned into hunger and his already thick cock stiffened into a staff that aimed unerringly at her.

She was not a prude, but hell, this was sexually at its most raw. And she apparently liked raw.

Who knew? All her boyfriends up to now had been friendly, flaky men who spoke in full sentences and never, ever growled. And yet one hairy, horny grunt from this guy and her nipples tightened while everything else went liquid.

Not a prude, then. Apparently, she fell more into the slut category because if he made a move on her right then, she wasn't exactly sure what she'd do to stop him. First of all, he looked like he could overpower her in a heartbeat. Second, the moment he'd offered her his mocha latte, her knees had gone weak and her lust spiked. When the hell had she developed a caveman fetish?

Insane!

But she wasn't a beast to be ruled by her hormones. And she certainly wasn't going to jump a near stranger, no matter how ripped his abs or how much he stared at her. Good lord, she'd never been the center of such focused attention. Need rippled off those sculpted pecs, it vibrated in the air between his broad shoulders and her tight breasts, and it seemed like he wanted her so badly it was hard for him to form words. But how was that possible? All he'd done was answer the door...naked.

She took a breath, startled—but not surprised—to find it thick with musk. His? Hers? Who knew?

Get a grip!

She momentarily flashed on what she could grip and struggled to restrain a near-hysterical laugh. She was not a woman who thought things like that. Not in the usual course of the day. So she closed her eyes and lifted her latte to her lips. Damn, he made a great cup of coffee. The honey added just the right amount of sweet.

Focus on the essentials: caffeine and sugar.

That's when he spoke. Two words: "no" and "leave." Well, that was par for the course from the men in her life. They'd act one way, then say the opposite. Get her revved, then disappear. Give her a latte and then order her to leave. All he needed to do now was invite her to move in, then break up with her and he'd be just like her ex.

But unlike what she'd done with her ex, she refused to leave. Her father needed his help, and so she would be stubborn. At least until she got a fuller explanation from him. One that included two-syllable words.

"So," she ventured when the silence stretched too long between them, "do you remember me?" She certainly remembered him. Linebacker for the football team with a crazy streak. She hadn't gone to high school here, but she'd spent a few summers being rejected by his clique while listening to tales of his antics. Everyone had talked about the stunts he'd pulled running wild in the state park. According to the gossip, he'd jumped from tree to tree the length of the park. He'd raced the train and won. He'd swum the river when it was still clogged with ice.

Blah, blah, blah.

What she remembered was him finding ways to keep her away from the group. He stopped people from talking to her, he hosted parties in places she couldn't find, and he never did anything but give her the cold shoulder. And where the great Mark Robertson went, everyone else—but her—followed. Which meant she had two very lonely summers thanks to him.

He was a dick of the first water…except for that one amazing, incredible, life-altering night. But she refused to think about that. Ever.

She grabbed onto the cruel memories now. In her mind's eye,

she lined up every time he'd turned away from her and used them to ice her hormones. She was here to get her father's journals, and she'd be damned if he frightened her away with his hard muscles and his manly lust.

"I'm Julie Simon," she said clearly. "You have my father's journals, and I need them."

He blinked at her, his brows narrowing enough that she noticed a long scar along his forehead. *Probably from tripping while racing a train,* she thought sourly. Though, damn, that looked like it had been a scary wound.

"Your father?" he said, his voice gravelly and bedroom sexy. His eyes drifted closed and he spoke as if he were just waking up from a really beautiful dream. "Julie."

She shivered at the unexpected timbre of his voice, laced with both yearning and pain. "Er, y-yes," she stammered, feeling way off-kilter. "My father is Professor John Simon. You've been working with him. Helping him with his computer system for his research. He said you had—"

"I don't." His voice was clearing, going from bedroom sexy to just radio mellow.

She huffed out a breath, irritation doing little to cool her lust, but every tiny bit helped. "He gave you his journals to digitize. I'm going to transcribe them for him while he's in the hospital."

His gaze sharpened. "Hospital?"

"Yeah. Heart attack. Bypass surgery a couple days ago." She kept her answer short, not wanting to relive the frantic midnight phone call from her mother or the drive from Chicago to Saginaw, Michigan, when her life was already in so much chaos. But considering the circumstances, her boss had given her leave from work. Then she had that anxious wait through the surgery while she, her mother, and her younger sister went slowly crazy from too much bad coffee and too little news.

"He okay?"

She nodded. "He's lucky he collapsed at the café in town. He got CPR immediately and then was air lifted to Saginaw."

She fell silent while he studied her face. His eyes narrowed, and the intensity kicked up in their dark blue depths. She hadn't thought anything about the man could be more raw than what she'd felt earlier, but his scrutiny made her uncomfortable. Like he was reading every curve and hollow on her face for way more than she wanted to reveal.

Then he set down his coffee with a hard *click*. "You are worried."

"Of course—"

"But not too worried. You believe your father will be fine."

Two complete sentences full of two-syllable words. Quite the improvement. Maybe now he'd put some pants on. Meanwhile, she watched him curve his mouth into a slow smile.

"I'm glad he's going to be okay."

Hard not to soften when he spoke in those bedroom tones. "So am I. But by tomorrow he's going to be bored. I was sent here to get his journals."

He frowned. "I gave them back a while ago." His gaze shifted from her to a large calendar on the wall. It was a *Dilbert* one, full of cartoons about working in the cubicle jungle. And it was on the wrong month. "What day is it?"

"Tuesday." Then when he stared at her in confusion, she got more specific. "June second. Do you need the year, too?"

He slowly shook his head as he walked over to the calendar. "I've been asleep for three days."

What? Holy shit! "Are you sick? Do you need to go to the hospital?" That would explain a lot.

"What? No." His voice was emphatic, but given that he was still staring at the month of May, she wasn't convinced.

"It's not normal to sleep for days on end." She kept her voice neutral, but was ready to dial 911 if he showed signs of delirium or something.

He swallowed, then carefully switched the calendar over to June. "It is for me. Lately." Then he stood there glaring at the new *Dilbert* image. "I woke up a couple times, I think, but fell right back to sleep."

"For three days?"

His gaze cut to hers, and in those dark blue depths, she saw a haunting despair—like a man staring down the barrel of a gun. And now she remembered what had drawn her to him as a teen. Even back then she couldn't look at that much pain without reaching to comfort him. But she only got one step closer before he stiffened and turned from her.

"I'm suddenly starving," he said, his voice settling into a forced cheer. After the husky tones from a few minutes ago, this was downright irritating. "Want something to eat?"

"No, thanks."

He crossed to a large refrigerator and pulled it open. A big T-bone sat in the center as well as a couple more cuts of beef, plus milk and a surprising number of fruits and vegetables. Given that her refrigerator contained an expired tub of yogurt and a crappy bottle of wine, she had to be impressed that Mr. Caveman kept a well-stocked kitchen.

"You sure?" he said, his voice becoming cheerier with every word. "I've got plenty."

"No, thanks. I had a burger on the way up."

"Ugh. Fast food." His tone held all the contempt of a celebrity chef. Meanwhile, he pulled out two steaks and threw them on a plate. His movements were efficient as he poured on a home-made marinade and set them aside to soak. Then he grabbed a variety of leafy greens, tomatoes, and God only knows what other vegetables for an amazing salad. Just watching him work was a de-light, especially given the way his muscles rippled as he sliced and diced.

The steaks went into the oven right before he started sautéing some kind of mushroom and onion mixture. *Oh, hell.* It smelled amazing, and her stomach rumbled. That burger had been a long while ago. He heard it, of course, and his eyes cut to hers even while he stirred his mixture.

"I was rude earlier. Please, let me make it up to you with some decent food."

She swallowed. Damn, she was tempted. Hot guy who cooked like a dream? Sign her up! But she knew the truth of him from high school. Someone who was mean to the outsider as a teen didn't grow up to have a generous soul. It just didn't happen, no matter how well he cooked or that she could play "name the muscle" on every part of his body.

"I just need those journals," she said. "Then I'll get out of your hair."

"I told you, I don't have them. I digitized them, then gave them back..." He glanced at the calendar. "Eight days ago."

"They're not in our cabin."

"Sure, they are. You just don't know where to look."

Actually, she did. With nothing else to do those two lonely summers, she'd learned her dad's "filing" system by heart. "They're not in the cabinet beneath the desk. They're not in the pile behind his lounger or beneath his bed. They're not in the pile by the toilet or the cabinet next to the coffee—there's just car magazine crap."

He turned and frowned at her. "Are you sure?"

She glared at him while desperately trying not to admire his profile. Muscled thighs, taut butt, washboard abs, and that dusky erection that had yet to shrink down. "Yes," she bit out. "I'm sure."

"Huh." He turned back to his sauté pan. A moment later, he sniffed the air. Apparently, he could smell when the steaks hit the right temperature because he quickly pulled them out of the oven. Then, he set them on two plates and poured the contents of the sauté pan over them. Next came the salads with a homemade dressing, of course, plus two glasses of lemonade that was probably homemade, too.

"Join me," he said. "Then I swear I'll help you find your father's journals."

Well, hard to deny him when he was acting so polite. And when everything smelled so divine. Then her stomach growled again, which had him smiling at her. God, he even had a dimple on his left cheek.

Unfair!

A normal woman would cave gracefully. She would smile and nod prettily while she joined him at the table. She might even offer to decant the wine or something. But Julie wasn't that smooth. Instead, she exhaled a reluctant breath and closed her eyes.

"I will on one condition," she finally said.

"What?"

Couldn't he guess? Hell. She opened her eyes and looked at him. He'd just put the plates and glasses on the table. He stood there—full frontal—looking as clueless as any child. But he was adamantly *not* a child.

"Could you please—for the sake of my sanity—put on some pants?"

He blinked at her. Two full blinks, then he looked down at himself. Yup. There he was in his full, woody glory.

She didn't realize a man could blush with his whole body. Truthfully, she'd never had the opportunity to see it happen so clearly. Golden brown turned mottled red. And the dusky wood? That even purpled a bit.

He made a choked sound, deep in his throat, and then his hands dropped to cover himself. Where before he'd been confident and manly, suddenly, his eyes were wide and his cheeks were bright red.

Adorable.

He gave her a quick nod before he dashed past her into the hallway and downstairs. Even his ass had turned pink. And wasn't that going to feature in her fantasies for years to come?

Julie smiled as she settled down at the table to wait for Mr. Pink Cheeks to return.

Chapter 3

*W*hat a bitch!

Mark pulled on his jeans, cursing Julie the Priss with every burning second of embarrassment.

He knew he was being irrational. What was a woman to do when a man opens his door stark naked? Squeal and run away? But for her to stand there and have an entire conversation with him while he was naked and erect? Had she been enjoying the peep show? Or did she just live to make him feel like an idiot?

She hadn't changed a bit from high school. She'd spent two summers here with her father after her parents' divorce, and the whole time, she'd turned her nose up at the uneducated hicks who lived in Gladwin. He'd done everything his adolescent mind could think of to attract her attention. Ridiculous stunts, feats of daring that could have gotten him killed. But all she'd done was turn her back on him as she buried herself in some book. Years later he learned that she'd been working for her father, doing research for his cultural anthropology papers. Not surprisingly, folktales about shape-shifters ran strong in this area. But that didn't ease the burn of rejection.

He had hated her until that one night when lust had overcome reason. One glorious summer night when all the awkwardness was gone and they'd been just a girl and a boy under the stars. Until his bear had to surface and ruin everything. Like it had today.

Why the hell had his grizzly decided on her of all people? It really needed a reality check because the last person who was ever going to let him between her thighs was Julie Simon. But did the grizzly listen to logic? Of course not. Even as it grumbled inside him for looking foolish, it still urged him to go back upstairs. To cook her food and feed her with his own fingers. And then, when she was fat and slow from eating, he could bend her over the table and impregnate her.

Moron grizzly.

He needed to get those journals and get her out of his home. The longer she stayed here, the longer it would take to get her scent out of his brain. And his bear would not be distracted as long as he could smell her.

With that in mind, he booted up his computer to make a digital copy of her father's files. Normally, that would take about five seconds. But he spent ten minutes trying to find a spare USB flash drive to load it on. He found one in his desk. It was shaped like a teddy bear with a goofy grin on his face and a tiny pinhole through his heart. A holiday gift from Tonya, who specialized in graveyard humor. Everyone knew he was likely to die in the next year—probably with a shot to the heart—so why pretend otherwise? Mark had laughed for ten minutes when he'd received it. Carl, their alpha, had stormed out of the room in a dark fury.

That was three years ago. Now that his death was ticking ominously close, the thing just depressed him. So he loaded the flash drive with the files and headed upstairs to give it to his high school nemesis. He found her sitting as regal as any queen at his kitchen table, food untouched.

"Something wrong?" he asked, his stomach twisting painfully in his belly. Damn, he was hungry. But the cramp faded beneath the purr his grizzly let off the moment she came into view.

She jolted and frowned. "No. Should there be?"

He gestured to the untouched meal. It pissed him off that she wouldn't deign to eat food he'd prepared. "Steak too rare?"

"No. I was waiting for you."

It took a moment for him to process her words. She'd been waiting because normal people ate meals together. They didn't swallow it down the moment food appeared like a starving bear. "Oh. Um. No need. Go ahead. It's probably getting cold."

"That's what microwaves are for."

He winced at the idea that she'd nuke his cooking, but didn't comment. He joined her at the table, forcing himself to sit down like a human being. The animal in him wanted to nuzzle her until she was pinned against a tree.

"Eat," he said. Suave…not.

She smiled uncertainly at him then picked up her fork and knife. "That's a nice tee. Is that a band?"

He looked down at his shirt and tried not to sigh. Did she

really think Nathan Fillion was in a band called *Spectrum*? "No. It's a TV show."

"*Spectrum*? I've never heard of it."

"It's not a real TV show."

"What?"

He looked at her and tried to find an easy way to explain a crowd-funded web series based on actors who played in a fake TV show called *Spectrum* but everyone knew was *Firefly*. "It's a science fiction show big in fandom."

"Oh. Maybe I can rent it."

"Good luck with that."

She looked up at him sharply. He didn't blame her. It wasn't a real TV show, but he didn't have the wherewithal to explain just then. And she still wasn't eating. "Don't you like steak? I can fix you something else."

"No. I..." Pink tinged her cheeks. "I was just waiting for you—the host—to eat first."

"What? Oh." He scrambled to hack off a hunk of his meat and shove it into his mouth. Had he lost his ability to function in polite society or had he never learned? Either way, he'd been watching to see her reaction to his cooking and not paying any attention to his food.

One bite, though, fixed that. Hunger gripped his belly, and it was all he could do to force himself to chew. Meanwhile, she cut off a dainty corner of her steak and popped it into her mouth. Her eyes widened with surprise, and then slipped partially closed in delight. Then, best of all, she released a low murmur of appreciation.

Now that was the reaction he'd been waiting for. He might be three-quarters feral, but he could still cook.

Grinning, he set to his meal with relish. Part of him wished he could slow down and appreciate his own cooking, but after three days, he was starving. If he were alone, he'd make another steak, but he didn't want to leave her even to go across the room. So he ate everything in front of him, pausing long enough to grab the bowl of leftover salad and inhale that. And yet through all that, he kept his attention on her. He watched her take precise bites and chew them daintily. He studied her every facial expression, watching for those seconds when she savored the taste of something. And God forbid she grimaced. If that happened, he would snatch away her food and make her something better. Something that hadn't sat cooling for fifteen minutes while he'd dressed.

But she never did. She liked what he'd given her, and that delighted his bear to no end. Especially when she ate every bite and sat back in her chair with a contented sigh.

"That was incredible."

"Did you want something else? Dessert, maybe?"

She chuckled, a low sound that rumbled down his spine straight to his groin. "After that? I'm so stuffed, my lungs don't have room to breathe."

Fat and slow, his bear thought. *The perfect female.* The man looked away rather than give in to the lust surging through him. "I made cookies."

"In your sleep?"

"No. Before I went down to work. I keep a stash on hand for programming marathons."

She titled her head. "Is that what you do? You're a computer programmer?"

She didn't know? That was refreshing. Everyone here knew what he'd created and why. "Um, yeah," he answered. "I wrote a hunting game that's become popular. The player can be the human hunter or the animal." And if the player happened to be a shifter teenager, then the game helped keep some of the hunting urge at bay.

"You can play the animal? Like the one about to be shot?"

"Yeah, but in my world, the bear can win. Or the wolf, cougar, or moose."

She blinked. "Moose?"

"Big hooved animal with dangerous antlers."

"I know what a moose is," she said with a laugh. "I just didn't think people would want to pretend to be one."

"Neither did I, but market research told me otherwise. So I programmed it and people have been buying."

"Good for you," she said.

"Thanks." It was good for him and for most shifters who needed to take the edge off. Sometimes being human got to be too hard, but it wasn't convenient to strip down and go animal. So he created a virtual forest for were-creatures to run wild. To hunt and kill digitally as a way to settle the instinctive need.

And it worked, especially for him.

Sadly, it hadn't done jack shit lately. The need to go grizzly was too strong. But he comforted himself that it was helping others and would continue to do so long after he was put down.

If only he could create a virtual mating program. He'd populate it with her and have at it until she was completely out of his system. But some things couldn't be done digitally, and this was one of them. Which meant for her own sake, he needed to get her out of here.

With that thought in mind, he passed her the teddy bear flash drive. He lingered too long with his fingers caressing hers until she drew back, a blush staining her cheeks. Stupid bear was still trying to claim her. "This has all your father's journals on it."

"Cute!" she said, but then she frowned as she saw the pinhole. Tonya had even managed to paint the puncture red somehow, but you had to look close to see it. Julie was and her face showed it. "Well, isn't that gruesome?"

She didn't know the half of it. Meanwhile, he tried to distract her.

"I don't have your dad's actual journals. If they're not in your summer cabin, maybe they're back in Ann Arbor. No offense to your father, but he's not that neat a man."

"Definitely not for most things, but he's obsessive about his journals. And I already checked his regular home. That leaves the summer place." She frowned at the teddy bear, obviously thinking hard.

"Did you find his tablet?"

She looked up. "Tablet? My dad's old school. He'd still be using a rock and chisel if he could."

Yes, that was definitely her father. "I set up a Surface Pro for him last year. Got it loaded with the right software and he loved the stylus. Find that and you'll find all his stuff."

She shook his head. "There wasn't a tablet anywhere. Just his desktop."

That old dinosaur? It was too heavy and too big to misplace. "I'm sure you'll find it."

She nodded slowly. "Yeah. I hope so." Then she glanced out the window. It was only late afternoon, but it was already getting dark. Summer storm coming in fast. "I better find it soon or it's going to be one sucky trip back to Saginaw."

He looked at her sharply. "You're going to drive back tonight? Why?" Damn it, his words came out as a growl.

"Because my father is waiting for his work, and he gets cranky if he doesn't have it."

"Your father is an adult who probably needs to rest. Plus, he'd rather his daughter live through the night than crash on the way to the hospital."

She arched a brow at him, the look both classy and arrogant. "You think I can't drive in a thunderstorm?"

"I think you've probably had a dozen hours of sleep in the last week." She was beyond beautiful to him. Something about a lush woman with curves everywhere made him salivate. But even his bear could make out the smudges under her eyes and the slight droop to her shoulders. Plus, given how much food she'd eaten, he'd lay odds that it'd been her first good meal since her father went into the hospital.

She brushed him off with a vague wave of her finger. "I'll be fine. This meal has definitely revived me."

Bullshit. But it wasn't his business. If she wanted to drive exhausted to her father's bedside, who was he to object? He'd done his duty, gotten her the digital copies, and warned her against stupidity. What more could he do? He was just standing up to say good-bye when completely different words came out of his mouth.

"At least let me help you find the journals. That way you can get on the road before it's dark."

She stood when he did. "No need. I'm sure I'll find them under a blanket somewhere." She didn't sound like she believed it, but was willing to hope.

He meant to leave it there. He'd give her the respect of making her own decisions. But different words came out of his mouth. Again. "I have to go into town anyway," he lied. "Your father's cabin is on the way."

"No, it's not," she countered. "It's on the other side."

He shrugged. "I don't get out much. Let me keep the illusion of having a social life."

She frowned at him, clearly trying to figure him out. He let her look. Hell, his bear loved it. Practically wanted to preen at her stare. "Are you trying to be chivalrous?"

He grabbed the keys to his truck. "Is it working?"

"Not since the Middle Ages."

That was completely untrue. He knew many women liked a man with knightly virtues. Unfortunately, he was as far from a man in shining armor as it was possible to get. "Look," he finally said. "I like your father. He'd kill me if I let anything happen to you."

"I just need to find the journals. And his tablet."

"And I need to get out of this house. Sometimes I feel like I'm going to die in my basement cave." Truthfully, that was his plan. Then he gave her a wicked smile. "You might as well give in gracefully. I'm going to follow you anyway."

"Very well," she finally said, then gifted him with a sweet smile. "It's like coffee and a good meal made you into a completely different man."

She had no idea. Question was, how long was the man in him going to last?

Chapter 4

*W*rong. *Very wrong.*

Mark stepped into the cabin—Julie's father's cabin—and immediately knew something was off. She'd opened the door, struggling with the rusty lock while he'd been looking at the clouds and wondering how long they had before the rain hit. Well, really, he'd been trying to distract himself from looking at her ass as she navigated the disaster that was her father's gravel driveway and rickety front porch. She'd been talking about packing too quickly and that she'd forgotten any type of rain gear. And then right after she'd pushed open the front door, that overwhelming sense of wrong hit him.

Immediately, he pushed her aside, stepping in front of her as he scanned the dark interior.

"What—"

"Shhhh!"

Thankfully, she took his hiss to heart and immediately quieted. He extended all his senses and wished he were in his grizzly form. He could detect so much more that way, but what he gained in awareness he lost in mental acuity. So he would remain human and protect her. But, damn it, he couldn't figure out what was wrong.

First, all the normal outdoor sounds were there. Chirping birds, rustling underbrush, even the distant bark of a dog. So nothing dangerous outside, at least as far as Mother Nature was concerned.

That meant the problem was inside. He reached behind him to flip on the light. The cabin flooded with electrical light. He heard the normal low hum of the appliances, saw the steady light on the DVR showing the time, and smelled the acrid scent of stale tea mixed with Julie's slightly floral scent.

"You came in here earlier?" he asked in a low voice.

"Yeah. Before I went to your place. What's the matter?"

"Shh. I'm trying to figure that out."

She started to move around him, but he jerked out his hand, keeping her back. She could have pushed it, ducking under his arm or objecting, but she didn't. Smart girl. Meanwhile, he advanced a step farther into the room.

He'd been here dozens of times over the past few summers. He had a key interest in her father's research and had made a point of becoming friendly with the man. Everything looked normal for Professor Simon's home. Casually messy, but not unhealthy. There was the living area front and center with a stack of *National Geographic* magazines scattered next to the recliner. To the right was a den that had a desk facing the window and an ancient computer setup. The door into the room was open so he could see that nothing looked odd there. In the kitchen, mail was set in a neat column on the counter—probably Julie's doing—and a crumpled bag of fast food had been tossed into the half-full trash.

"Do you see anything weird? Different or out of place, maybe?" he asked her.

"No. And you're freaking me out."

His hackles rose at the fear in her voice. His bear hated making her afraid and wanted to rip into whatever it was that made him so nervous. "Something feels wrong."

"Can you be a little more specific?" There was an edge to her words, part sarcastic, but more anxious.

He didn't bother answering. Instead, he paced to the master bedroom. Slowly pushing open the door, he saw an unmade bed and a heap of laundry. Bathroom looked typical, too, though Julie had obviously been in there. There was an open toiletry case, and she'd thrown in toothbrush, comb, etc.

"You were packing things. For your father?" He needed to keep her talking. Her anxiety was cranking up his bear.

"Yes. And it looks exactly as I left it."

Okay. So whatever was off probably hadn't happened recently. He left the master bedroom and climbed the stairs to the upper loft. This was the guest bedroom, and his nose twitched at the dust. No one had been up here for a while. Except that whatever was wrong lingered here, too. A scent too subtle for his human nose.

She climbed up the stairs behind him, flicking on the stairway light as she went. He looked to her. Even on high alert, he couldn't resist seeing the gentle bounce of her hair as she stepped into view. But that's when his eyes narrowed on something he hadn't noticed before.

"Stop!" he snarled, and she froze.

Pulling out his cell phone, he flipped on the spotlight, aiming it in the corner nearest the stairs. There was a thin layer of debris there, but it had been disturbed. Possibly by a large boot.

"What is it?" she asked.

"The dust has been disturbed."

She frowned at him. "Seriously? That's a dust bunny that hasn't been cleaned in, like, a year."

"It's not shaped right."

She gaped at him. "Did you get a degree in forensic science after high school? Criminology? Or have you just watched a little too much *CSI*?"

He ignored her, turning his phone so the spotlight ran over the entire floor. He couldn't see a pattern. Maybe someone had been up here. Maybe he was just seeing things. "I trust my instincts."

"Yeah, me, too. And mine say yours are crap." She was teasing him. He could tell by the tilt of her head and the slight lilt in her voice when she spoke. He wanted to respond. Hell, he wanted to flirt and cajole and a zillion other things. But something overrode his mating instincts, and that was serious. So he didn't respond to her overture, and eventually she huffed out a breath and headed back downstairs. He couldn't blame her. He hadn't given her any reason to think he was anything but nuts. But something *nagged* at him.

Taking one last look around, he lingered on a framed picture

of teenaged Julie and her father. She looked young and fresh
there, kissing her father who still had his hair. It matched his
memory of the girl he'd once tried to attract, but it also struck
him how young she had been. Cheeks flushed, eyes bright, and
everything about her alive. The present-day woman wasn't as
bright. She was tired and disillusioned, her tone occasionally edg-
ing toward bitter and that saddened him. The woman had lost
something that had made the teenager so vibrant.

Seeing nothing more of interest up here, he followed Julie
back to the main level. She'd gone into the den to stand with her
hands on her hips as she glared at the floor.

"Dad said his journals were right here," she said pointing to
the untidy desk. "But I looked everywhere."

He followed her in, and his nose immediately twitched.
"Don't move," he ordered. She was disturbing the smells.

She gaped at him. "Is this some sad kind of come-on—"

"Out."

She blinked. "What?"

"You're confusing the scent." He edged to the computer and
bent over to sniff the chair.

"Did you forget to take your meds?" Her voice was part exas-
perated, part teasing, but he could tell she was losing patience. So
was he, but not with her. There was a puzzle here, and he didn't
like where it was heading.

So he abruptly crossed back to her side. Even though he towered over her, she didn't do more than lift her chin and arch
one eyebrow. It was an impertinent look, and his bear loved the
challenge in it. The man didn't need the distraction, so he bent

down, picked her up, and then set her just outside the den door. She squeaked in protest, but he moved quickly and with all his strength. By the time she had the breath to object, he had already gone back to the desk.

He was on the hunt now. It didn't matter that he was in his human form; some things were universal to both man and grizzly. In this they were the same: a singular focus when in search of prey. And since the man had vetoed chasing her, the bear allowed him to search for the unknown *wrong* that was threatening her.

Mark bent down, pushing his nose into the seat of the chair. He smelled Professor Simon as clear as day, but there was another scent. A man who liked onions and something else. Something very *wrong*. It was faint, but it was so unsettling that it turned his stomach.

He moved around the room trying to zero in on the rancid smell. It was strongest at the desk, and he returned there only to rock back on his heels in disgust. He needed another opinion. Someone who would take him seriously even if he was going crazy. He pulled out his phone and hit the third speed dial for his alpha. Maximus Carl Carman answered before the second ring.

"You okay? Where are you?"

Mark winced at the worry in his once best friend's voice. "I'm at Professor Simon's cabin. You know where it is?"

"Yeah."

"I'm here with his daughter. I need…" *How to phrase this exactly? I need you to come sniff a chair? I need you to tell me that this is not some weirder stage of going feral? I need you to take Julie away from me before I forget myself and pin her against a wall?* In the end, he settled on the most general of statements. "I need your opinion."

Silence. Then understanding. "You need my opinion *there*."

Trust Carl to get it in one. "It's a weird smell," he said. "Almost like…" His voice trailed away. He hadn't even thought of it until the words had started to form on his lips. "Before."

"Does this have to do with the missing kids?"

A month ago, three shifter kids had gone missing—two wolves and one grizzly. Carl had saved two of them, but the psycho who'd been experimenting on them had disappeared along with a mysterious cat-shifter. The Gladwin grizzlies had been on alert ever since, but no new information had surfaced. At least not until now when Mark thought he might be smelling something similar. Hell, it was hard to tell. Meanwhile, his alpha was waiting for an answer.

"It's not the same as what I smelled then," he said, trying to compare this to the thousands of scents that had been in the bastard's lab.

"But you suspect something."

Maybe? He took another whiff. "It may be nothing."

Carl didn't need anything more. "I'm on my way. But as long as I have you on the line—"

Mark thumbed off the phone. The last thing he needed was a bunch of useless how-are-you-doing questions. And anyway, Julie was clearly getting impatient where she stood in the open doorway.

"Mind telling me what's going on?"

"Someone's been here. Someone who isn't your father."

"Could be a lot of someones," she said. "He interviews people here. Plus, I think he's seeing a woman." She didn't sound upset by that. Her parents had been divorced for over a decade, so she'd had plenty of time to adjust to the change.

He nodded and pointed to the living room. "Dot doesn't come in here," he said. "She was in the living room and kitchen." And bedroom, but no use telling her that little tidbit. "This is different. Whoever it was did something with your dad's computer." Probably sat here while he either copied her father's research or downloaded something onto the computer. He wouldn't know until he could get his own equipment here to check it out.

Julie wasn't buying any of it. "Look, this is all very dramatic and everything except for one thing. Nobody cares about my father's research. He tracks folktales. His own department barely cares."

"I care," Mark answered honestly. The man was looking into the anthropological background of shifter legends. Since Professor Simon was fully human, he called them fairy tales, but Mark knew there was a lot of truth to those old stories. From the moment the man had started asking about shape-shifter tales eight years ago, Mark had kept an eye on her father's work, hoping to find an answer to his own particular problem. But he'd only gotten personally acquainted with the man three years ago when the professor had started focusing on the bonding rituals between shifters and their mates. Fascinating stuff for a guy who was desperately trying to keep his sanity, hoping for an answer in the old tales. But he had to admit that Julie had a point. He was hard pressed to see how anyone else might be interested.

Julie shook her head. "It obviously gets really boring up here. I'm going to go pack my father's bag. You want to go sniff any more chairs? Have at it." Then she pointed a pert, pink fingernail at him. "And find his journals!"

Mark barely resisted the urge to give her a mocking salute. Meanwhile, the first smattering of rain began. A few isolated plops on the windowpane, but it was all the warning they were likely to get. A deluge was coming soon.

"Oh, shit," he cursed.

"What?"

"The rain. It'll wipe any evidence outside."

"What evidence? There's been no crime!"

There was no convincing her, especially since he had plenty of his own doubts. But any hope of finding an answer outside was about to be washed away. So he headed for the door, resisting the urge to slip into his grizzly form. Last thing he needed was for her to get spooked and shoot him.

"Stay inside," he ordered. "And stay out of the den."

She rolled her eyes as he stepped out onto the porch. It wasn't until she shut the door on him that he realized his mistake. It came at the same moment he heard the lock snick shut.

"And don't lock me out!" he said through the door.

An evil chuckle was her only response.

* * *

Julie watched through the window and grinned as Mark sent the closed front door a frustrated grimace. She wondered if he would try the lock just in case. He didn't. Instead, he narrowed his brow and turned his intense stare to the edge of the front porch. Then he seemed to draw into himself a bit, hunching his shoulders as he took slow, predatory steps forward.

She knew that stance, recognized his focused intensity. One summer night years ago, he'd stalked her like that. He'd hunted across her body, holding her gaze as he touched her in ways she'd never dreamed were possible. And the things they'd done that night had set the bar for every lover since.

She hated seeing that look again because it reminded her that he was done with her. He hunted something else, and she was nothing to him now. But even more, she hated that it still made her insides go wet. Even her damned nipples tightened, so she turned away in disgust. Let him bang on the door. She was done with him and this horrible little town in the middle of nowhere. She'd find her father's stupid journals herself and leave before dark. And given the coming storm, it didn't look like she had much time.

She made quick work of packing a small bag of her father's things. All he needed was basic toiletries and a pair of pajamas. The real work would be after he left the hospital. Her whole plan was to gather up his work and then transport him to her tiny apartment in Chicago instead of coming back here, which is what he wanted. But that meant she had to find his tablet and journals.

Though she'd already searched once, she did a thorough check of every nook and cranny of his bedroom and bathroom just in case. It didn't take long. Then she headed out to the main living room, annoyed at herself when her gaze went to the window and the rainy landscape. She was looking for Mark, of course, and she found him rounding the corner of the house at a slow lope. His hair was plastered to his head, his tee was a second skin, and, boy, did she love the way his ass moved, especially in wet jeans. But it was the size of him that attracted her more than anything. Big guy, all muscle, and that raw physical power thrilled her. She was a big woman and he'd carried her to the door like he was lifting a stack of mail. So easy and she'd been weak kneed in response.

She was so busy reliving that moment that she didn't even realize there was another man at the door. Not until Mark stopped rounding the cabin and jumped up on the porch.

It took her a while to figure out the newcomer was Carl, Mark's best friend, whom everyone had laughingly called Mr. Max for no apparent reason. The last time she'd seen him, he'd been a teenager with a warm laugh and tired eyes. He'd grown since then until he was taller than Mark, plus he'd added a beard, which would probably look sexy to another woman.

They were talking in low voices when she stepped near the window. Mark's nose flared, and he turned to look right at her. She hadn't made a sound, she was sure of it, but he acted like he knew she was right there. And his eyes—damn, those dark blue laser beams—cut straight to her, daring her to keep him out of the cabin.

She was moving to unlock the front door even before she realized her intention. What happened to her self-control? But she'd started the motion now. It would be silly to relock the door. So she opened it, her gaze going unerringly to Mark. But he wasn't the one who spoke. Instead, it was Carl, his expression warm as he smiled at her.

"Hello, Miss Simon. Do you remember me?"

His eyes were still tired, and there was an extra layer of concern in them whenever he looked at Mark, which was often. But there was also a contentment in his voice, which was new. Well, as far as she could remember. Her attention had always been on Mark.

"I remember you, Mr. Max," she said. His nickname came uneasily to her lips. She wasn't sure she had the right to use the familiar form of address. Apparently, she did because his smile widened. "I always liked the way you said that," he said. "Like I really deserved the title."

"It's a title?" she asked. She hadn't known.

"Only for some. Feel free to call me Carl." Then his expression sobered. "I was sorry to hear about your father. Dot has kept me up to date on his condition. I know he did fine with the surgery, but is there any other news?"

She relaxed with his easy chatter. Where Mark had always been intense, it was Mr. Max—Carl—who had tried to welcome her. "He's tired and anxious to get back to his research."

Carl shook his head. "He's like a dog with a bone, your father."

"Always."

Then there was an awkward pause in the conversation. Julie was standing directly in their path, blocking the front door, though it was clear they wanted to come in. And as always, she noted when Mark tightened his hands into fists. When his shoulders hunched even more. And when his expression became stubborn.

"Julie, it's not safe to be standing out here exposed like this."

She loved it when he sounded protective. The illusion that some man would actually think of her safety was a need that had burrowed deep inside her years ago. Problem was, there wasn't any real danger out here. He was making it up for some sick reason of his own. Probably because most women—including her—went liquid when he talked like that.

"There's no danger, Mark. There never was."

He growled at her, low and nearly inaudible. "There isn't time for this. You're muddling up the scent." The frustration was clear in his gravelly words.

She turned to Carl. "You going to smell the furniture, too?"

Carl shrugged, looking moderately embarrassed. "I guess so."

She blew out a breath, and with it went her resistance. "Anybody ever tell you guys you're freaks?" she asked as she stepped aside.

"All the time," Carl answered.

Her skin prickled as Mark moved past her. It might have been her imagination, but she thought she saw his nostrils flare as he went past. Almost as if he were smelling her. And she pretended he touched her arm to reassure her. He didn't. Or at least, if he did, it wasn't for her benefit. It was simply because he was so large and she was the complete opposite of petite. So he'd brushed against her side, and while she remembered caresses under the moonlight, the men went to sniff her father's office.

God, she was pathetic. How could she still be mooning after the same man eight years after he broke her heart?

She followed a couple steps behind as they went into the den.

Mark stood a step back, dripping on the rag rug, while Carl squatted down and inhaled the air around the chair. Then he looked up with a frown.

"You sure that isn't just…I don't know…bad pepperoni?"

"It's not," Mark answered, his voice clipped.

Carl rolled back onto his heels and looked around. "And his research is missing?"

"The journals are. My guess is they're with whomever copied his computer."

Unable to keep silent, Julie pushed into the room. "But why? He's not working on national secrets. He's an anthropologist with weird ideas about shape-shifters and magic potions in fairy tales."

She'd expected the men to nod and admit that she was right. Logic dictated that the idea of someone stealing her father's stuff was cuckoo for Cocoa Puffs. They didn't. Instead, they shared a long look that meant something she couldn't fathom. And, oh, how she recognized that expression. It was summers in Gladwin all over again where the teenagers knew something she didn't. And with that one look, they said, "You're not one of us."

"That's it," she said as she gripped the front doorknob. "Get out. Both of you." She wasn't an awkward teen anymore. She didn't need to feel inferior just because she didn't look or act like the locals. And she sure as hell didn't need to be excluded in her father's home.

"I know this is confusing," Carl said as he stood up.

"It's bullshit. I don't know if this is Gladwin's version of hazing or what, but…" She pulled out her most officious tone of voice.

"I'd like you both to leave please." She yanked open the front door.

It was a good act. She'd used it to great effect in the law office where she worked as a legal secretary. She'd cowed managing partners and obnoxious clients with that no-nonsense tone. And it worked on Carl. He nodded with an apologetic look.

"Thank you for letting us bother you, Miss Simon," he said. "I hope your father gets better soon."

Mark wasn't so easy. He looked around. "We still haven't found his research. He'll want that tablet."

"You probably hid it just to be a juvenile pain in my ass." It wasn't a fair statement. There was no evidence that he'd go that far in his sniffing psychosis. But who knew what quirks lurked inside that hot package?

Meanwhile, he dropped his hands on his hips, glaring at both her and Carl. "There's something wrong here," he stressed.

Carl seemed torn as he looked at her. "Can we at least help you look for the journals?"

"No," she said flatly. "He'll just have to be satisfied with the digital version." Then she pointedly stared at Mark, who hadn't budged. "Look, I'm leaving in the next ten minutes anyway. Whatever's wrong can rear its ugly head while I'm gone."

Which is when both men shifted awkwardly. Carl even went so far as to scratch at his beard.

Oh, hell. "What now?"

Mark jerked his chin toward the outside. She hadn't even noticed when the rain had become a deluge, but it was coming down in thick sheets of drench. Shit. No way was she making it to her car without getting soaked to the skin. "Fine," she huffed. "I'll wait until it eases up."

"Look at the driveway," Mark said. "Specifically, how far the mud goes up the tires of your car."

Her gaze shifted to her beloved blue Prius. Her little hybrid was both economical and good for the environment. And was sunk a foot deep into the swamp formerly known as her father's dirt-and-gravel driveway.

"Shit." She wasn't going anywhere in her car. "Is there a tow truck anywhere?"

"There is," Carl said slowly, "but it'd sink in the mud on the way up. I told your father he needed to pave that."

Her father would never spend the money required to pave the long, winding track that led to this cabin. He always said if it was ugly outside, he'd just stay inside until Mother Nature co-operated. Which was fine for an academic with no particular schedule, but awful for a daughter with plans.

She sighed and leaned her head against the door frame. She could hope that it would clear up soon. If it happened fast enough, maybe there'd be some daylight left. Except even as she had the thought, Mark pulled out his phone. A few punches later, and he turned the screen toward her.

"Radar says it's not going to let up any time soon. You're probably here for the night." He didn't look any happier about that than she did.

"Fine," she groused. "I'm here." There was food and electricity, not to mention a guest bedroom with that dust-bunny footprint. "But you two don't have to be. Good day, gentlemen."

Carl nodded and stepped out, but again, Mark refused to move. He just stood there while his pecs seemed to pulse with irritation. No wait, that was him grinding his teeth. "I'm not leaving."

She didn't have to answer because Carl turned to his friend. "There's nothing more we can do here. Whatever that was…" He gestured back toward the den. "It's long gone."

Mark didn't look like he agreed, but he didn't argue, either. After one last intense stare at her, he sloshed his way outside. Julie made a point of keeping back from him. She had no need for any more accidental brushes, real or imagined. And when the men stepped onto the front porch, she firmly shut and locked the door.

Done. Over. Mentally, she closed the drawer labeled "Mark the Fickle Bastard."

It took her ten minutes to realize that she'd heard only one truck leave. She went to the window, pulling aside the curtain as she searched the shadows outside. There he was, a shadowy outline squatting at the edge of the dry area of the porch. His body was so still he might have been a statue.

Was he sitting sentry?

She couldn't believe it. No way was he going to sit there all night long like a neglected beagle. Or a bizarre stalker. But how the hell was she going to get him to leave?

Chapter 5

It was going to be a cold, wet night, but Mark found a kind of peace in the chill. The days when he would be human were ticking away, so every sensation became special. Instead of cursing the icy wind on his skin, he cherished the sensation of exposed flesh unprotected by fur, of fingers heated by his breath, and toes that squished his soggy socks. Miserable, but even this was beautiful to a man who didn't expect to live to see the snow.

He heard her open the front door and step out onto the porch. She'd been watching him on and off through the window for the last half hour, and he'd wondered if she'd eventually come out to talk with him. He wouldn't if he were her. But then he was notorious for not giving a shit what other people did. She, on the other hand, appeared to have a softer heart.

"You're going to catch your death of cold out here," she said. She stood in the doorway, electrical light framing her lush figure. He remained in the shadows, trying to force himself to keep watching the grounds and not spoil his night vision by looking toward her. But he couldn't stop himself, so he turned and smiled.

"I'm pretty hardy."

"You're crazy," she said, staring at the deluge outside. "Nothing dangerous is going to attack me in this."

Except him. God, she smelled so good, he was already rock hard. Even with the wet in the air, he could smell her musk. Maybe even more so. Musk and something almost as good: hot coffee.

"I know you think I'm crazy," he said, "and, frankly, you're probably right. But I can't leave you unprotected." Not after knowing there was something so wrong out in the world. Something that had been inside the cabin.

She sighed as she joined him in the shadows, holding out the mug of coffee. "It's just my dad's cheap shit coffee, but at least it's hot."

He took it gratefully, sipping the brew fast enough that it burned his tongue. His earlier java hit was wearing off, and he appreciated the brain boost. Sitting here scanning the world made him engage too many of his grizzly senses. Caffeine would help keep him on the human straight and narrow. Especially since she'd doctored the drink perfectly.

"Milk *and* sugar," he said. "You know how to tempt a man, don't you?"

She sighed when he'd expected her to chuckle. He turned to study her face. Sure, his joke had been feeble, but it hadn't warranted that frown on her face.

"You do know I'm a paralegal, right? And I've worked on criminal cases."

He had no clue what she was getting at, so he didn't respond. Eventually, she would start talking again. It took longer than he expected, but in time, she leaned against the siding and spoke.

"This wouldn't be the first time a man has created a situation just to get a girl to trust him." Then she twisted her gaze back toward the den. "Though it certainly is the weirdest. And risking pneumonia is new."

"I rarely get sick," he said. He heard a rustle to his right and shifted to hear better. A possum hunting for trash. They never cared about rain. He relaxed again, though he kept his gaze on the darkness. "You should go back inside. Thanks for the coffee."

"What if I'm attacked through the back door? What are you going to do then?"

"I set a couple traps in the back. I'll hear it before you're in any danger. Plus, I do a perimeter check periodically."

He heard her sharp intake of breath. "You put traps in the backyard?"

"Just at the edge of your property line."

"And what if I decide to go for a walk?"

"I'll hear that, too, and join you. They're not lethal traps, anyway."

"Do you even hear yourself? Just how long do you plan to hang around?"

"Until you leave in the morning. Then I'll set up a security system before your dad gets back."

"A security system? My dad will never pay for it."

That was true. Her father was the original penny-pincher, though not for the usual reasons. He just never wanted the hassle of people invading his space for any reason. Pave the driveway? Why bother? Watch for intruders? He didn't have anything anybody would steal. Except, of course, he did. He had no idea how valuable his research was to a feral like him.

He heard her shift uncomfortably behind him, and he cursed himself for getting lost in his senses again. It was yet another sign that the animal was too close to the surface. He routinely forgot the ebbs and flows of human interactions.

"Look, it's no trouble," he said. "I've got plenty of money. And if I can keep you and your father safe, then it's well worth it."

"Safe from what?" she huffed, thereby taking the conversation full circle. She thought he was nuts. He *was* nuts, but not that way.

"I'm not abandoning you again," he finally admitted. "Not when it costs me so little to keep you safe."

"Again?"

Oh, hell. Had he said that out loud? That's what came from trying to manage human interactions. He forgot himself and said the wrong things.

"So you do remember me," she said.

Her words startled him enough that he turned to face her, no matter what it did to his night vision. Did she seriously think he'd forgotten the best night of his life? The one time when animal and human had been so perfectly in accord that everything aligned in absolute synchronicity? And that she had been the center of that miracle of perfection? Until it had unbalanced. Until he'd lost control and tipped into beast, then run in terror.

"Yes, Julie," he said dully. "I remember you."

"And you're not going to abandon me again. Not going to run off howling into the night and never speak to me again for eight years."

He stiffened. "I did not howl."

She pursed her lips, apparently thinking back. "I really think you did."

Well, he might have made a loud animal kind of noise. But grizzlies did not howl. "Maybe it was more of a roar."

"It was…" She chuckled. "It was perfect. Until you didn't come back."

"And I've been waiting eight years to apologize for that."

She arched her brows, her expression disbelieving. "You haven't thought twice about me since that night until I showed up at your door today."

"Not true." So incredibly not true, she had no concept of how large a misconception that was. "But by the time I got my act together, you'd already gone back to Chicago. And you didn't come back the next summer."

"And Gladwin is so backwards there aren't phones. Or even the postal service."

He sighed, knowing she was right. "I was a teenage boy. We don't communicate well."

"I have news for you, Mark. You don't communicate well now."

Well, that was certainly true. "Look, I was a dick. I knew it wouldn't work between us, so I just…let it go."

She took a breath. "Why wouldn't it work between us?"

Hell, she was like a dog with a bone digging at him. But he couldn't give her the truth. He couldn't tell her that he was shifter and she was human. Normally, that was just the ticket for someone like him. A strong shifter had to mate with a pure human or risk a child who was too animal. But even back then he'd known he was on the path to feral insanity. There was no saving him, and that night showed him how far gone he already was. After all, it had taken him more than a month to return to human. Even his father had given him up for dead.

So he landed on a lesser truth and hoped she'd leave it at that. "You lived in Chicago with your mother. I lived here."

"That's your excuse? Long distance?"

He groaned. "To a kid that's a big deal. Plus, you're rich, and your dad's a professor. My dad didn't graduate from high school, and I ate stuff I killed, skinned, and cooked myself."

She arched her cocky, impertinent, damn sexy eyebrow. "That espresso machine looked pretty expensive. Not to mention whatever security system you're—"

"That's now," he said, hating that his face had flushed hot. "Back then we had nothing."

"And you think I care about that? And if you think a professor makes a lot of money, then you clearly don't understand academia."

God, why wouldn't she just give it a rest? "Like I understood that then," he said. "Look, I'm trying to apologize. I was a dick and I'm sorry."

She was silent for a long moment, but in that time he heard her breathing relax until she released a slow sigh. "You're forgiven.

Hell, you're right. We probably couldn't have made the long-distance thing work."

"You had a boyfriend in Chicago, anyway."

She jolted. "Whatever gave you that impression?"

"I saw your prom picture, remember?" She'd worn a crystal-blue gown that had hugged her curves, showed cleavage that made his head spin, and made him wonder if she ever made it past the front doors and into the dance. If he'd been her date, he'd never have let her out of his car.

She laughed. "That was my cousin. Trust me when I say you were the only one in high school."

"What? That can't be true."

She shook her head. "You jocks always think life is an endless party of cheerleaders and casual hookups."

"And you geeks never lift your nose out of your books long enough to see that there's a whole world around you waiting to be enjoyed." What made that accusation even funnier was that he turned out to be the biggest geek of them all. He was the one who hid himself in software coding rather than face what he was becoming. By all accounts, she'd gone on to create a good life for herself in Chicago.

Meanwhile, she was silent for a long while, but in the end she said one word. "Touché."

He grinned. "You seem to have ended up okay."

"You're the one with the expensive espresso machine."

"It is my favorite appliance, but you can have it after I die."

"Yeah, thanks," she drawled, having no idea that he meant it seriously. Then she straightened off the wall. "So we're good, right? Teenage drama all cleared up? I'm not holding any grudges, you're not obligated to sit on my front porch and freeze to death. So go home, Mark. Live long and prosper."

He smiled at her, glad to get at least this tiny mark off his soul. "We're good." Then he drained the rest of the coffee and handed it to her. She took it from him, and their hands touched. Fingers entwined and held. Heat transferred from her to him and back again. Lust slammed into him hard, but he didn't move. He wouldn't break this moment of accord. Not even when she blushed a fiery red and pulled back, coffee mug in hand.

"I'm glad I woke you up this afternoon," she said.

"I am, too."

Then he nodded to her and took off toward his truck. She stood there on the porch watching him as he started up the vehicle and drove it down the long driveway. He didn't know how long she waited. He watched her until the rain hid her from sight.

Then he drove a few hundred yards farther until he found a good spot to park his truck. Five minutes later, he was doing another full-perimeter check. Fifteen minutes after that, he was back on her porch, tucked into the shadows as he waited for something *wrong*.

Just in case.

Chapter 6

Julie's first thought was, "That's a strange car alarm." It sounded just like birds tweeting loudly outside her window. Then she cracked her eyes, realized she was up in the loft of her father's cabin, and that it really was birds out there making that racket. Well. Guess she'd been living too long in the city if she couldn't recognize the sound of real birds.

She rubbed her eyes and stretched, feeling achy in every part of her body. Last night, she'd dropped like a rock into bed only to spend the night fighting erotic dreams. She didn't even want to acknowledge the identity of the man who had done such delicious things to her, but it was hard to deny the wet hunger she felt now.

Nothing that some coffee and a cold shower wouldn't fix, she thought as she pushed out of bed. She found a pair of pink cat slippers and a matching bathrobe, all left behind from high school and about two sizes too small. She'd always tended toward large, and years of office work had done nothing to make her slim. Downstairs, coffee was an exercise in fumbling, but she managed, and soon the scent of caffeine was filling the room. But it wasn't ready yet, so she stepped to the window and looked out.

The world was still wet, but drying quickly. In truth, everything looked washed clean, and so she opened the front door and stepped out to enjoy the beautiful morning. She never got air this clean in Chicago. Even her apartment windows were sealed shut to keep out the smog.

She moved forward, only to be startled by a dark shape to her right. She spun toward it, her heart beating in her throat. Then her shock ratcheted up even further when she saw what it was. Or *who* it was.

"Mark! What the hell?"

He was crouched in the corner, his eyes burning golden in the…she would have said morning sunshine, but he was in shadow. And yet his eyes were so clear to her. He was looking at her with that intensity that was as frightening as it was thrilling. And then his nose twitched and he opened his mouth. It took him two tries before sound came out, but eventually he croaked out a word.

"Coffee?"

"Uh…yeah. God, Mark, what are you doing here?"

He didn't answer, and she already recognized the state he was in. It was the same version of him that had answered the door naked, and it wasn't that he was half asleep. Crouched as he was, he looked like a wild animal. His clothing was plastered to his skin, and his hair was slicked straight down. As if he'd been siting just like that all night long, through the rain until the morning dried everything on his body. Without him moving an inch.

His nose twitched again, and she was grateful she'd made a full pot.

"I'll get the coffee." She started to move back to the kitchen but stopped long enough to look again at him. Whispers of the night's eroticism filled her mind, showing her exactly what she'd dreamed about. A man who was more animal than human. More elemental than reason. More thrilling in his raw power than anything in the civilized world. She cleared her throat, suddenly uncomfortable with the lust pounding through her blood. "You're freaking me out, you know," she said. It wasn't true. She was freaking herself out, but she couldn't admit that to either of them just yet.

He didn't respond, so she went for the coffee. Two mugs, poured and sweetened with shaking hands, and then she carried them carefully outside. Except when she stepped back onto the porch, he wasn't there.

"Mark?"

She looked frantically around, disappointment blooming inside her belly. What the hell? Had she dreamed him? Was she going insane?

She moved to the porch railing, setting the extra mug down. Then she sipped her own drink, letting the heat burn her tongue and hopefully wake her brain cells. A sip. Another. Five more before she decided she'd gone insane.

Then he appeared on her opposite side, stepping up onto the porch in near silence. She didn't see him until he reached for the mug on the railing.

She squeaked in alarm and jumped back. And when her heart steadied to twice its normal rate, she blinked hard and stared. Yup. He was still there and still looked like rumpled man in a handsome bad-boy kind of way. Even his morning beard looked sexy, and the lust-crazed part of her brain wondered where on her body she'd like to feel a beard burn.

"I thought I'd imagined you," she said. She'd certainly dreamed about him.

His gaze never left her even as he drank his coffee. He was gulping it down, and she wondered if he'd just burned his throat.

"What are you doing here?" she asked again.

He pulled the mug away enough to speak. "Perimeter check." His voice had that gravelly texture to it that hit her happy button on a visceral level. He should do morning radio.

She blinked. Of course. That's where he'd been when she went to get coffee. "And it was quiet all night, wasn't it?"

He shook his head.

It took her a moment to understand what he was saying. *It hadn't been quiet?* But she hadn't heard a thing. She hadn't even known he was there. Her gaze strayed to the woods around her. What sort of evil creature had been out there? And was he just making it up to freak her out?

"I scared it away," he said.

"I didn't hear a thing."

"I smelled it. Before it made the property line." He looked out at the woods and growled. Yes, an honest-to-goodness growl. "It's fast. Couldn't catch it."

Well, he was clearly pissed about that. Affront to his manhood and all that, which actually made her smile. This whole thing was bizarre, and she had no idea if this was all in his head or not. But either way, he believed it. He'd stayed out here in the rain all night long just to protect her. She had to be grateful for that. Not to mention being filled with all sorts of inappropriate feelings about being cherished.

But that was crazy talk. It had to be. Mark was the definition of flaky: über-Neanderthal one moment, über-rational the next. It was all part of his here again, gone again pattern, and she wasn't getting sucked in. But she also couldn't leave him sitting out here.

"Come inside, Mark. It's cold out here." It might be the height of summer, but early morning after a rainstorm could be downright chilly.

His gaze traveled out to the woods, clearly worried.

"What's the plan, Mark? You going to sit here day and night protecting me? Don't you think you'll collapse or something?"

"You're leaving today." He spoke the words in his clipped way, but she thought she heard a plaintive note underneath. As if he didn't want her to leave, but couldn't express it normally. Lord, when he was in this state, it was like dissecting the words of a toddler.

"Come inside," she said firmly. "I need to call the hospital about my dad. You need to warm up. Why don't you call Carl?"

Mark's eyes widened at her words, then he looked up at the sky. "It's morning now. Carl will be awake." He rubbed a hand over his face as he inhaled deeply. "Caffeine's kicking in."

She nodded. "Do you want me to call Carl for you?"

"No." He straightened and pulled out his phone. "I'll text him. You call the hospital."

She smiled and held open the front door for him. "There's more coffee if you want."

"I definitely want. Though how your father can drink that swill is beyond me."

"He's a man of plebian tastes."

She said the word as a test. Would he understand the word "plebian"? It was a kind of measure of how much brain function he had just then. Apparently not enough because he frowned at her, then looked away, a flush staining his cheeks.

"Right," he said, his voice flat. Still in Neanderthal mode.

She stepped inside, leaving the door open. He was staring hard at his phone, working the buttons slowly, but eventually picking up speed. What was he doing? How *sane* was he? Was she safe?

That last was the question that lingered in her thoughts. Given what she'd already seen of Mark, she guessed he was some form of bipolar, which meant that he could go nuts on her at any point. She ought to be grateful he'd gone into protective mode instead of aggressive. Which meant task one would be to get away from him.

But she didn't feel threatened. Logic told her that she couldn't trust that. But it also pointed out that Carl seemed to trust him completely. Wouldn't he know if she was in danger? Wouldn't he say something if his friend was off the rails?

She watched Mark labor over his text message. He was certainly not fast with the thing, but to be fair, neither was she. And he had larger thumbs than she did. Made it harder to text with ease.

Sighing at the chaos in her own brain, she finished off her mug of coffee and set about filling her stomach. Her father had to have *something* in here. But what she'd seen last night had been dismally thin.

She found some bread that hadn't gone moldy and decided on her favorite breakfast of champions: peanut butter and jelly. She made one for herself, another for Mark. She also found her cell phone and called her sister for the update. Dad was doing fine. They'd find out today if could go home. She chatted while eating, keeping half an eye on the tense man on her front porch. For most of her call, he stood poised on the front step, but just before she hung up, he abruptly spun around and loped around the side of the house.

Probably another perimeter check or something. She finished with her sister and her own sandwich, then went out to her car to grab her suitcase. She'd been so tired yesterday, she hadn't bothered fighting the rain to bring it in. But now it was morning and she needed to take a shower, not to mention setting up her stuff here. If Dad was discharged today, he'd be coming to this cabin—he'd insisted—so there was no point in her going back to the hospital. She'd do more good stocking his refrigerator and doing his laundry. God only knew when he'd last washed his sheets.

She'd just pulled on shorts and a tee when she heard Mark come into the cabin. She couldn't deny the tightening in her gut at the sound of his heavy footfalls, but was it excitement or fear? What was the prudent course of action?

Annoyed with the whirling in her thoughts, she headed for her bathroom to brush her teeth and delay seeing him for another few minutes. But it didn't help. All she did was churn through the same questions while her anxiety climbed another notch. Was she safe? Was he right, and there was really something dangerous out there? Why was she so attracted to him? Would he flip out on her?

She rinsed. Spit. Grabbed a dry towel and cleaned off. Then looked in the mirror and choked on her scream.

He stood right behind her. Large. His eyes intense and a little wild. And his whole body dwarfed her by many inches on all sides.

"Mark?" she managed in a quavering voice.

"You're trying to make yourself afraid of me," he said, his voice low and dark.

It was on her lips to deny it, but the way he was looking at her made her hold back the words. He wasn't angry. He was hurt. "You confuse me," she said honestly.

"I'd never hurt you."

She swallowed. The way he said it, she believed him. But what was happening here was beyond weird. "I don't know what you're thinking. I can't read you and—"

He stepped closer, blocking her in on all sides. Her words ended on a squeak of alarm, but the rest of her heated at his nearness. She didn't even have room to turn to face him. Then he leaned forward, his hands gripping the counter on either side of her. And his head bent down slowly to press lightly against the side of her head while the heat of his body seeped into her backside.

"I thought about you," he said softly. "All night, I thought about when we were teens. About what we did and how I wanted you." He swallowed. "And how I blew it." He closed his eyes, inhaling deeply. "I'm sorry, Julie. I was an ass."

"I already forgave you yesterday. And long ago."

She felt his body pressing against her, hot and hard. Not just his muscles, but the thickness between her butt cheeks. Their clothes did not mask his erection, and she was both terrified and aroused by the feel of him right there.

"I know I'm crazy," he said against her temple. "I know I frighten you."

She wanted to deny it, but couldn't.

His eyes remained closed as he spoke, and so she watched the tight muscles of his face and felt the slow, steady pressure of his body against hers. "I'm dying, Julie. Literally. I won't see the New Year. Probably won't make it to October."

She jolted. "What?" The idea that this vital man would be gone in a few months was completely alien to her. He was too strong, too much *here* for him to ever be gone. It made no sense. She started to twist to look at him, but his hands shifted to grip her hips and hold her in place.

"Don't move. Let me explain."

She stilled and waited, but he didn't speak. Eventually, she huffed out a breath.

"You're supposed to be explaining."

He chuckled, sounding so casual that she felt whiplash again. He was laughing off his death as if it were a minor technicality. "Turns out there isn't much to explain. The…disease doesn't matter. We've tried everything."

"Like…chemo and stuff?"

"Stuff," he said as he pressed his lips against her forehead. He didn't even seem to know he was doing it. He just rolled his head lightly and pressed his lips against her. "I've known for years. Fought it for years. Eventually, it just wins and all I'm left with is regrets." He swallowed. "I'm sorry I hurt you back then."

She leaned her head back. She didn't want to. The situation was too weird. But his shoulder was so broad it just worked for her to settle against the shelf of his collarbone. And she felt *safe*. Insane to feel that way, but she did. "You're forgiven already. Geez, let it rest."

At least the pieces now fell into place. The mood swings between Neanderthal and über-logical. The casual disregard of the normal rhythms of life. If she thought she was going to die in a few months, she sure as hell would sleep whenever she felt like it, day or night. She'd drink whatever coffee she wanted and answer the door naked. Who the hell cared?

God, he was dying? The very idea made her tear up. He couldn't be. He was too alive.

"Don't cry," he whispered. "Not for me."

"Why not for you?" she asked.

She met his gaze in the mirror and tried to blink away the blurred vision. His eyes looked sad and hungry all at once. His hands tightened on her hips.

"Please don't cry," he said. "You're too beautiful to cry."

The way he said it made her heart ache. He really thought her big bones and huge boobs were beautiful, not to mention her belly. She took a deep breath and tried to gain control. Not only of her emotions, but of where they stood in the bathroom and what he was doing. He was holding her pressed against the sink, stopping her from touching him while he all but laid himself along her back.

"Mark," she said as she straightened up. "Mark, step back."

He didn't want to. She saw it in his eyes. But he pulled himself back from her, and she used the space to turn around. To face him. To look into his eyes and feel everything she'd been fighting.

"Mark…" she whispered, wishing she knew the right words to say. His gaze caught and held on her mouth, but he kept his body away. And then she knew it wasn't words he needed. And though her mind screamed warning alarms, the rest of her just went with the emotions churning within her.

"This disease you have. Is it…contagious?"

He shook his head. "You can't catch it. I wouldn't endanger you that way."

"Is there any way at all for me to catch it? Like, is it AIDS or something like that?"

His lips twisted into a wry smile. "I'd never endanger you that way," he repeated. "There is nothing we could do that would make you sick."

She nodded, smiling slowly. "I'm still making you use a condom."

He nodded, clearly not processing what she'd just said. Then a second later, his eyes abruptly widened. His body jolted then stilled into wariness. "I—Julie—"

"You weren't the only one thinking about that time when we were teens. I spent the last night dreaming about making love with you." She cast her voice light as a way to hide the intensity of the emotions she felt. "I figure if you're horny and I'm horny, we might as well—"

"Pity fuck?"

Her chin jerked up. "Not on my end. Is that what it would take for you to want me?"

Again the blink, but this time he pulled back. "What? Jesus, no! God, I've wanted you since I was sixteen."

Well, that couldn't possibly be true. Otherwise, he wouldn't have disappeared back then. He must have read the doubt on her face because his hands tightened into fists.

"I told you I was an idiot. I ran off because I freaked out. You were too much. I wanted so much. I was afraid for us both, and so I ran. And I kept running for six weeks."

She frowned. "What?"

"I stayed in the woods for six weeks starting from that night on. By the time I calmed down…by the time I got back to me, you'd already left."

She couldn't fathom it. "Six weeks? No way."

He dipped his chin. A quick jerk down and to the side. He was embarrassed. So she touched his cheek, bringing his gaze back up to hers.

"I never know if you mean what you say. Six weeks in the woods?"

He shrugged. "Call me the original mountain man."

"Because you freaked out."

"Yup."

"I don't know whether to be flattered or pissed that my naked body could freak someone out for six weeks." A month and a half. Because of what they'd done together? Which hadn't even been the full deed. Sure, she'd gotten off—multiple times because he gave the best oral sex she'd ever had. But when it had come time for more—for him—he'd gotten all weird and run off. "Tell it to me one more time. You freaked out why? And disappeared for how long? No bullshit."

He took a deep breath. "I wanted you so bad, Julie. I knew if we did...*it*, I'd never stop. I'd change and I'd be..." He rubbed his hand over his face. "Just trust me on this. You were here for the summer and no more. There were things you don't know about me. I just couldn't control it around you, so I ran. It's hard at that age not to...you know...hurt a girl."

She searched his face, reading the truth in his expression. She'd thought he'd run off because he couldn't face being with her that way. He was saying it was because the feelings were too intense. That he had wanted her too much. That was so...so...*wonderful*. Adolescent love is so pure and passionate. She'd always missed having a teen love like in books where the need was all encompassing. Sure, she'd felt that for him, but she had no idea about him. Or rather, when he'd disappeared, she figured he didn't feel the same.

What if she'd gotten it all wrong?

She stroked her hand up his jaw, a slow caress over clenched muscle and bone. "So we both got confused back then. Care to try again?"

He looked at her, need hot in his eyes, but his body remained still. "I can't promise anything, Julie. I'm not going to last much longer."

She swallowed away the lump in her throat. "I can't promise anything, either. I'm just here because of my father. I have a life in Chicago. Just got a good raise."

"Congratulations."

"Thanks." She stepped closer to him. Then she dared press a light kiss to his lips. He clung to her, pressing against her, but not taking over. And certainly not devouring her the way she remembered from when she was sixteen. So she pulled back. "Mark, I'm an adult and I don't do this ever. But I know I want to. Let's fix what we broke years ago. Let's do it right, okay?"

He nodded, a quick jerk of his head. "Okay."

She smiled. "So—"

She didn't get more words out. He picked her up, swinging an arm beneath her knees. He was so amazingly strong.

She squeaked in alarm and threw her arms around his shoulders while everything inside her went liquid with pleasure. To be held like this—so easily—and carried straight to her bed was like all her romantic and erotic fantasies coming true. Then he set her down gently without strain. And while she sank into the mattress, he came down over her. She lifted her face to his while his eyes roved over her. So intense. So hungry.

"Mark…" she murmured, gently stroking her finger across his mouth.

He licked her finger, a long curl of his tongue before sucking her inside. Meanwhile, his hands began to move, rolling up her waist onto her breasts. He held her in both hands and pinched her nipples. Even through her bra, she could feel the sharp bite of it, and she gasped in pleasure.

"God, yes," she whispered. "Do that again."

He paused a moment, then abruptly grabbed her tee, lifting it off her in one quick pull. A moment later, he'd unhooked her bra and set her free.

"God, yes," he echoed as he looked at her breasts. Then he grinned. "I'm going to do that a lot."

Chapter 7

Sometimes the stars align, the fates are kind, and everything is exactly as it ought to be. Mark looked at Julie's body and knew that God had given him a precious gift. If he didn't take it with joy and gratitude, then he was a damned fool.

She had said yes. He hadn't even truly asked, but she had said yes, and so he'd carried her to bed. And now she sat before him with her glorious breasts pink and perfect in front of him. He could hardly breathe for that sight. But as he looked, she flushed hot and tried to pull in to herself. She curved her spine away from him, and her eyes canted down and away. He'd seen this reaction before, knew it for the idiocy it was, and he'd be damned if he let the most beautiful woman be awkward about who and what she was.

"Mark," she murmured. "I know I haven't exactly got a runway model figure—"

"Stop," he said. Then he closed his eyes, inhaling her arousal but also the acrid bite of shame. Not of what they were doing, but of her own body. "From the moment I noticed girls, I thought I was weird because I hate delicate or thin."

"What?"

He opened his eyes, then he pressed a tender kiss to her cheek. But this close to her, he had to lick her as well. And so he tasted her lightly, nibbling along her jaw while her breath stuttered hot and moist against his skin. "I liked curves." Actually, he *loved* them. "Size and strength are beyond attractive to me."

She bit her lip. "Strength?"

He pulled back enough to set his hands on her shoulders. "Strength," he repeated as he gripped her. "I'm not going to hurt you if I get enthusiastic." He grinned. "And I am extremely enthusiastic."

Her expression softened into gratitude, and that pissed him off. Damn it, he didn't want her to be thankful that he liked her. He wanted her to understand that her body was amazing. To know core deep how beautiful she was.

"Strength," he repeated as he squeezed her frame. "And curves." His voiced dropped into a low, growling purr as he looked at her breasts. They were large and flushed, her nipples dark and tight. He shifted his hands again, glorying in the weight of them, the sheer size. Oh, the things he was going to do with this much flesh. He pushed them together and groaned at the sight of all that cleavage. He wanted to bury himself there between her lush mounds. And he was going to lick, suck, and nip every sweet inch.

He gently took hold of her arms and pushed them above her

head until she could grip the headboard. "Don't move," he said. "If you can resist."

"Why not?"

"Because I want to enjoy this." He looked into her eyes. "I want you to know I love this."

He leaned down, taking the time to smell her skin. She had an artificial lemony scent to her that was probably shampoo or soap. But this close, he could smell the orangey citrus that came from her and the tangy spice of her arousal. He scraped his teeth across her flesh, tasting salt and sweet in equal measures.

His hands shaped her, and he adored how she overflowed even his massive palms.

The dark berries of her nipples called to him, so he tasted them next. They were large enough to tease with tongue and teeth, and she squirmed. Her back arched and her breath came in short, tight gasps he nipped her. But she groaned in hunger when he sucked. And best of all, her scent grew stronger each time he fondled her breasts.

It was amazing, and he could have stayed there for hours. But another scent drew him downward. Pepper and spice and everything nice. He managed her shorts with ease, pulling them off her while she twisted toward the bathroom.

"Condom," she gasped. "My toiletry bag."

He didn't like thinking of why she was prepared, but didn't have a reason to object. It's not like he could protect her in this way, not with his bear clamoring to impregnate her.

Rather than give voice to his feelings, he spread her legs to look at her glistening center. "In a minute," he growled against her thigh.

"Don't for— Ooooh!" Her exhale was low and lusty, and he grinned as his fingers slid in and through her wetness. There was so much here, and her scent made him dizzy. Roasted nuts soaked in pepper. He'd never tire of that.

He pushed his fingers inside her, playing first one, then two, then stroking all over as he learned what she liked. Leaning in, he wedged her thighs farther apart. He had broad shoulders, and he wanted total access to the feast before him.

"Don't let go," he said merely to prolong the moment. Her aroma swirled through his senses like a delicious fog. He felt drunk on it.

When he couldn't hold back any longer, he went in. This wasn't just about tasting her, though God knew he adored that. This was about hearing her gasp when he pushed against her clit. About the way her body trembled when he sucked. Her thighs were strong where they gripped his shoulders, and he imagined her legs pulling him in deep. But the most amazing thing of all was the way her hips lifted toward him. While he feasted on her, she strained for him, undulating against his mouth and making keening sounds.

He kept it going as long as he could. He let her cool off while his fingers opened her. Then he surprised her with a sharp push with his tongue or a low growl. He liked the way the vibration of his sounds went through his mouth to her. And he loved that she responded with noises all her own.

There was one sound he particularly loved. A high gasp, nearly inaudible. But he knew if he kept the tempo quick, her breath would shorten into pants that soon became a scream.

So he did it. He pinned her legs open with the weight of his arms, and he set to licking with determination. This was something his bear adored and so he let it slip its leash enough to feast. Her sound started low, but quickly built. Higher. Hotter.

Nearly there.

Then he bit against her clit.

Her body convulsed. His fingers were inside her, pulled tight and high. And, oh, yes, she screamed.

What a glorious sound. What a sweet sight—her body quivering before him. And the scent had his bear roaring in hunger, licking every inch as she orgasmed beneath his tongue.

What a woman!

His bear was taking over, the mating imperative coursing through him. This is where he'd lost it so many years ago. He felt the prickling of fur on his skin, the thickening of bone, and the extended length of his tongue as he laved her body. He was shifting. As a teenager, he hadn't the control to stop it, but he was a man now. He would not terrify her.

He wrenched himself away and stumbled blindly for the bathroom. He had to stay human.

His bear ears heard her breath ease before a slow purr of delight.

"I've never…No one…" Her voice was tentative, but he heard every word. "You really do love that."

Language. Words. They came slowly, but hidden from sight, he could shape his mouth as a human. He could beat the bear back enough to stay a man. "I do," he said. "I love. Your taste."

He heard her shift on the bed. "Are you getting the condom? It's right—"

"Stay there!" The words were more of a bark, and he heard her still. "I'm trying not to explode. Just give me a minute." He closed his eyes and breathed deep. Her musk continued to fog his mind, but it was muted in the bathroom. His joints settled. The fur receded. His paws settled into hands.

"Mark?"

Talk to her. Keep human. "Can we…" He swallowed. "There's a position I really like."

"Yeah?" There was curiosity in her tone. Maybe even delight.

"I like being able to touch you while I'm in you."

"Um, okay." She clearly didn't understand, and he didn't have the mental capacity to explain.

Instead, he focused on stripping out of his clothes. He found the condoms and suited up with shaking hands. And when he returned to her, she was still in that boneless, dreamy place. So pretty. So lush. What he wouldn't give to see her like this every morning, year after year.

She smiled at him and pushed herself upright. "Mark," she said, and there were layers of meaning in his name that he hadn't the brainpower to understand. He heard tenderness and longing, maybe. Or maybe he just needed to hear it.

Swallowing, he stepped into the sunlight. Her eyes widened when she saw him. No part of him was small.

"I'll go slow."

She blushed a fiery red. "Don't hold back for my sake."

He grinned as he stepped to the edge of the bed. And when they kissed, he felt an urgency from her that startled him. As much as his blood thrummed in his ears, demanding faster, harder—*now*—she seemed to want it, too. And now. And...

Wow.

His hands were shaking when they separated. And when he looked in her eyes, they were dark with hunger, the air spicy with lust.

"Don't be gentle, Mark. I don't want gentle."

Thank God because at that moment, his bear broke free. He kept his body human, but only barely as he flipped her on the mattress and lifted her to all fours. Then he pushed his hand between her thighs. She was slick as she opened for his penetration.

"Cant. Go. Slow," he panted.

She arched her spine, offering herself to him.

He impaled her. A single deep thrust and her silken heat surrounded him. Her passage squeezed him—gloriously tight—and he leaned down to scrape his teeth across her shoulder.

"Mine," he growled.

She keened, high and tight. Not in pain, but in that prelude to orgasm he'd learned a few minutes ago. He wanted to touch her as he had before, but the bear was in charge. It was pounding into her, thick and hard. His hands gripped her hips, holding her in place.

So good. The slide and the pull. Squeezing inside. Drawing deep. All to the sound of her gasps. Shorter. Tighter. Higher.

She bucked beneath him, writhing in pleasure. He rammed as deep as he could before doing it again and again.

And then she did it.

A high squeak that became a scream.

She convulsed around him.

He exploded inside her. All of him pouring into her.

Wild. Primal.

Julie!

Chapter 8

Julie was floating on a sea of happy afterglow. She'd had sex before. She'd made love with men she thought she'd spend the rest of her life with. And once, yes, she'd gone to bed with a man she'd guessed wasn't the right one but wasn't exactly sure. Oddly enough, that had been her best sexual encounter...until now.

Now there was a whole new bar for excellent sex. Like in a whole new galaxy.

They were spooned together with his arm wrapped around her while she tucked tightly back against him. She'd probably passed out there for a bit or been catapulted to a new universe. Either way, she was barely conscious except for her state of satisfaction. And the way he kept pressing sensuous licks to the back of her shoulder made her smile from the inside of her soul.

Didn't men fall asleep after sex? Apparently not Mark, who punctuated his licks with a kiss while gently stroking her arm. Long, petting strokes. She purred in delight. Wow, a whole bunch of new noises had come out of her this morning. She might have been embarrassed, but he'd seemed to enjoy her every sound. Which had, in turn, encouraged her to let herself go without restraint or self-criticism.

How freeing was that?

She sighed happily, stretching her fingers out to entwine with his. He caught her easily, then tugged on her thumb for some unknown reason. She giggled, and he did it again while rubbing his chin stubble across the back of her neck.

Rough and exciting.

"Aren't you sleepy?" she asked. After all, he'd been up all night.

"And miss this? Hell, n—"

His word was abruptly cut off at a clanking noise from outside. It was quick and quiet, but he went rigidly still.

"What?"

"Perimeter," he whispered.

He gently rolled her off him and padded to the window. She didn't hear anything anymore, so she relaxed into the sight of his gloriously naked body as he stood in profile. Roman nose, biceps better than a Marine's, and a stomach of rippling abs that made her mouth water. He'd cleaned up at some point, so the condom was gone, but his penis was still thick and partially erect. A good look on him.

While she stood there admiring his body, he flipped the latch, then pulled up the window. He probably wanted it to go up quietly, but nothing in this cabin had been oiled in years, so it opened with a shriek that made him wince.

She sat up. "It was probably just a raccoon or—"

Gunshots rang out. Three quick ones. If she hadn't spent a summer volunteering on the South Side of Chicago, she would have thought it was a car backfiring or something. But she knew that sound, even though it still took her brain a few seconds to believe it.

Gunshots? Here?

What the hell was a hunter doing this close to her dad's cabin?

She scrambled out of bed, heading for her clothes, but that was nothing compared to what Mark did. He shot her a single look, dark and angry.

"Stay here!" he said, and then he ran out the door. She hadn't even fully stood up when the front door banged open.

Her gaze shot to the window where she clearly saw the front yard and a flash of skin…Wait, no! She saw a freaking animal running across the front lawn. And not just a dog or a possum. A huge animal with dark fur that really, really looked like a bear. But it couldn't be that, she told herself. What would a bear be doing running across her lawn?

She stared out the window, looking for a hint of what she'd seen. Nothing.

Oh hell, she realized with a dull kind of shock. Mark had gone out there looking for God-only knew what. He'd set perimeter alarms to catch some vague idea of a bad guy, but he sure as hell wasn't thinking *bear*.

She had to warn him. He'd run out naked, for God's sake. Not even a weapon against the hugest creature she'd ever seen outside of a zoo. She pulled on her clothes as fast as she could manage while simultaneously shoving her feet into sandals. Like pretty flip-flops were going to be useful when tromping through the woods. But she wasn't going far. Just into the backyard to call for Mark.

She was already out the back door when she realized she didn't want to yell for fear of attracting the wild animal. But that was ridiculous, she told herself, striving for logic to calm her racing pulse. First off, wild animals ran from humans, right? Second, the thing had been in the front, not the back. But Mark had said the perimeter alarms were around the back of the property. So that's where he would be. So she could be as noisy as she liked, right?

"Mark?" she called, pitching her voice to be loud, but not a scream. "Mark, come back. I think I saw a bear."

She listened and thought she heard something, but who could tell? Thumps or wind? God, she had no idea what she was supposed to hear in the country. What was normal, what was Mark being a freaking moron.

Then she saw a flash out of her peripheral vision. Golden fur, the flick of a tail. A large cat? Were there cougars in Gladwin? She took a few steps closer, but couldn't see through the trees bordering the park.

"Mark!" she called as she headed to the back of the property and Gladwin State Park. "Mark, quit freaking me out. I just saw a huge cat. Where the hell are you?"

Bam! Bam!

Two shots in rapid succession to her right. *Damn it! Who the hell hunted in a state park?* She started running in that direction. "Hey!" she bellowed. "Whoever the hell you are! There are people around here. Quit—"

A dark figure came out of the woods ahead of her.

"Julie? Get out of here!"

She might have screamed, but she realized it was Carl in a red shirt running toward her with a gun out.

She frowned. "Carl?" She squeaked in alarm as he barreled toward her. Then she realized his shirt wasn't red. It was covered in blood.

Blood!

He ran fast, gesturing toward the house. She straightened, intending to get them both into the house, but then a dark thing blurred past her on all fours. It came from ahead and to the right, passing within a few feet of her as it ran toward the house. It was smaller than the bear she'd seen before and quick. She barely saw it when the rapport of Carl's gun deafened her.

Two shots, and the dark thing swerved.

Julie screamed and dropped into a crouch—like that would help her against a bullet—only to realize he'd been shooting past her at the blur. And what the hell was that thing?

It slowed and stumbled, landing awkwardly between a bush and the back of the house. Human-ish. Big for a man. It had dark patches of fur mottling its humanlike skin, and a muzzle for nose and mouth. And it didn't stay down for long. Between one breath and the next, the thing rose on all fours, and its hands were more like huge paws with dirty claws. Worse, it wasn't alone.

What? Her brain stuttered in panic when she saw a second of those things emerge slowly from around the side of the house. This one was smaller, meaner, and more…dog? Bear? Hell, she didn't know.

"Don't move," Carl said, his voice low. He'd moved closer to her, the sound coming from a couple feet away. But when she glanced at him, she saw him sighting his gun on…oh, shit. He was aiming to the right where the first thing had emerged from the tree line. This one looked the most human of them all. He—it—stood upright, but its eyes were crazed. Three of them, in a ragged kind of line from the trees to the house. They were looking at her and Carl as they edged steadily to her back door. No, wait. The injured one was heading to the house. The other two were coming at them.

Terror clawed up her throat, but she forced herself to focus. Now was not the time to curl up in a fetal ball. She had to *think*. She took a breath, trying to steady her racing heart and tasted blood on the air.

Carl.

She glanced at him. He'd closed the distance between the two of them. "How bad are you hurt?"

"Stay with me. I'll keep you safe."

"Not what I asked," she snapped. But, stupidly, she did feel better with his promise. Then she looked at his ripped shirt and the wound beneath. There was a jagged edge of claw marks across his chest. And though only the center slice looked deep, it was all bloody.

"I'll live," he said, his voice tight. Then he flipped her his phone. "Call 911."

He hadn't done that yet? Shit! She snatched up the phone, but it was protected. "What's the code?"

"Nine-one-one-one," he bit out, then he shot. Again with the deafening sound, especially since he was nearer her ear. But she'd been looking nervously at the…things, and the one crouching by her back door flew backward in an explosion of red. Yuck. But she wasn't upset that it was dead.

Fortunately, she didn't drop the phone. She quickly hit nines and ones in what she hoped was the proper order. But there wasn't time. As soon as the first one went down, the others attacked. They came tearing at them while Carl kept shooting. The things swerved and one stumbled, but they were fast.

Julie couldn't hear anything anymore. She was sure she was screaming, but she was deaf from the gun and the roar.

Roar?

The bear. The huge, black grizzly bear she'd seen in her front yard flew right by her, coming from behind them. It landed right in front of her with a thud she felt through the ground. But it didn't attack her. No, it went for the closest man-thing, mauling it with massive paws. God, it was so close. The thing had been within a foot of her, but now all she felt was the heat pouring off the grizzly's back. She jerked backward and tripped over her own feet.

Carl's gun ran out of bullets. He dropped down beside her and started dragging her backward, away from the house and the fight. And why the hell hadn't she been moving already? Because she'd been struck stupid by the sight of the bear ripping whatever it was into bloody scraps. And she'd thought *The Revenant* was gross. It had nothing on the real thing, especially when the beast was less than a foot away.

She crawled backward with Carl while he slammed another

clip into his gun. She risked a glance at the third creature. It was down and spurting blood from a couple bullet holes. So one dead by the back door, the other riddled with bullet holes, and the third was now mincemeat thanks to the bear. That meant they just had to get away from the grizzly.

But then Carl froze, one hand on his gun, the other on her shoulder as his gaze went to the tree line in the direction they'd been moving.

Oh, hell. There was something there. She had no idea what it was. Just a shadow of movement. But Carl pointed his gun at it, and she strained her eyes trying to figure out what he'd seen.

"Mark!" Carl abruptly barked. "Eastern tree line. *Mark!*"

She didn't see Mark. She looked all over, trying to find him even while she cursed herself for dropping the phone. Damn it, it was back there by the grizzly who had abruptly stopped chewing on the man-thing. The huge bear who suddenly stopped growling to look up and over. At the eastern tree line.

What the fuck?

Had it sensed whatever the shadow was? Or…hell…was it about to attack Mark? Mark who was naked and about to be eaten by this bear.

"Run, Mark!" she screamed. "Run into the house!" *And come back with an Uzi.*

The grizzly turned to stare at her, and she almost swallowed her tongue. Oh, hell. She started to scrabble backward, but she was shaking and terrified, and she couldn't get purchase on the grass.

"Over there!" Carl said, gesturing broadly to the tree line.

"Mark! There was something else over there!"

"A cougar. I think. I saw it earlier." God, she hoped she was wrong. The last thing they needed was a cat-bear fight.

Meanwhile, the grizzly's head swung to the eastern side of the property. Carl grabbed her arm and hauled her up to her feet. But at that moment, the bear looked back at them and slowly pushed up onto his back feet, growling the whole time.

It had been big before, but on its hind legs like that, it was terrifyingly massive. And even half deaf, she could hear its growl.

"Mark!" Carl yelled again, and even she could hear a note of desperation in his voice. "Mark! Check the perimeter. Go!"

Perimeter check? How about, "Go call 911 from the house"? How about, "Kick over a trashcan and distract the damned bear?" How about anything but a perimeter check?

She and Carl backed up together, moving slowly away as the grizzly towered over them. It didn't seem like it was about to attack, but what the hell did she know? And though Carl held his gun out, it was pointed to the side and down.

"Just shoot it!" she cried. She was as much a pacifist as the next person, but right now, she really wanted him to blow the thing's head off.

"No!" Carl bellowed, and she didn't even know if it was at her or at the bear. But there was fury in his tone, and she cringed from the force of it.

Which is when the bear lunged forward. She dove to the side, and Carl shot wildly at the ground, spraying dirt into the air. She landed on her butt, still scrambling backward, while Carl rolled to the opposite side. He came up on a knee, his shirt matted with dirt and blood, but his eyes were steady as he faced off with the creature.

Damn it, why didn't he just shoot?

The bear was almost between them now, maneuvering to separate them. Obviously sensing that Carl was the bigger threat, the creature's golden eyes focused there. Which gave her the opportunity to head away from them both. She wasn't exactly sure what she was going to do, but if she went off toward the back of the property, she might be able to draw the creature away from Carl.

So she backed up. No hope in getting to the house, but she was a fair hand at climbing trees. The grizzly was too big to climb up after her—she hoped—so that was her escape route. It was a stretch, to be sure, but she clung to it like a lifeline.

And while she moved backward to the closest sturdy tree, Carl remained eye-locked with the creature. He was talking, pitching his voice low and calm, his words making no sense at all.

"I'm not the threat, Mark. Take a big whiff. I'm bleeding. No danger to her. Go look for more of those things."

Oh, shit. Carl was a lot more hurt than he was letting on. Which meant that she had to act now. She was close enough to the tree, she hoped. And she really hoped that she wasn't about to commit suicide. She'd gathered a few rocks as she'd moved. All that she could see while inching herself backward. Gathering all her softball experience into her brain, she adjusted the heaviest rock in her hand and threw straight at the creature's head.

Score!

She tagged it right at the back of the noggin. She thought at first that even with the impact, the rock had been too light to make a difference. But then grizzly turned to look at her. Good…maybe. But she was working on adrenaline now, so she pitched the next and the next and the next.

Three stones in rapid-fire throws, all hitting him not because of her accuracy but because it was that freaking huge. And in case that wasn't working, she started screaming at it.

"That's right. That's me, you big bully. Get away from him!"

She thought Carl would take the opportunity to scramble away from the bear. At least he had a clear field to empty his clip into the creature's head. But instead of doing the intelligent thing, he started screaming at her.

"No, no! Julie, stop it! Don't upset him!"

Don't upset the thing-eating bear? Bullshit. It was pretty damned riled up already. So she whipped the last two stones in her arsenal at it, one of them nailing the beast right on the nose.

It roared in fury and finally abandoned Carl to go for her. Great!

Or not.

She gulped and tore for the tree, kicking away her flip-flops as she scrambled up the trunk.

Ouch, ouch, ouch!

The bark sliced into her hands and feet, but adrenaline kept her from feeling the worst of it. And even with her moving as fast as she could manage, she was still way too slow. She felt the creature's breath on her back as it roared again. And the tree shuddered as a single paw swiped at her feet.

It could have knocked her down. She was sure of it. But by some miracle, that massive paw hadn't connected with her leg.

It had simply slammed into the tree trunk, making the whole thing shudder. She swung herself up into the nearest branch, then half leapt, half hauled herself up the next. The tree swayed ominously, but it didn't break. And, damn it, there weren't any other branches higher up that could hold her weight. Which is when she chanced to look down.

The grizzly was standing up, two massive paws stretched against the tree about six inches from her feet. One good jump and she'd be toast. This close, she could hear its mournful lowing and see every pointy inch of its claws.

Damn, damn, damn.

But at least she'd gotten it away from Carl, right? She looked over, hoping to see the man scrambling full tilt for the house. That would be the intelligent thing to do. No such luck. He was running toward her, gun at his side, talking nonsense all the way.

"Don't make any sudden moves," he called. "Just stay there. And for God's sake, don't throw anything else."

"Are you crazy?" she bellowed. "Shoot it!"

As if the creature understood what she'd said, it turned its head and roared at Carl. The sound was a loud rumble that sounded a thousand times worse than any movie-made roar she'd ever experienced.

Carl stopped running forward, half stumbling as he gripped his bloody side. But his gun hand was steady as he aimed down at the ground.

"I'm not coming any closer, Mark. I got it."

Who the hell was he talking to? She didn't see Mark anywhere.

Meanwhile, the creature let out another furious roar, though not quite as loud as the last one.

"You're frightening her, Mark. Smell her. She's terrified."

Bizarrely enough, the creature did seem to sniff. It was probably just a natural predatory instinct, but still. A sniffing bear wasn't a ripping-her-out-of-the-tree-and-eating-her bear, right?

"You have to calm down. You have to remember who you are."

The bear turned to her, then, lifting its snout up in her direction. If she bent her knees, she could probably kick it. That would discourage it from coming closer, right? But she really didn't want to get her foot that close to the thing's mouth.

But what choice did she have? Any second now, the bear might decide to climb up for her.

"Don't move, Julie!" Carl said. "You don't understand what's going on. Just stay still."

A bear was about to eat her, that's what was going on. But she didn't argue. If he thought she should freeze, then call her Ms. Popsicle. And then—miracle of miracles—she heard the sound of a police siren in the distance.

Hallelujah! People with guns were coming. People who would actually use them instead of holding it to the side and putting bullets into the ground. She just had to stay alive until they showed up.

"You hear that, Mark?" Carl continued. "We're safe. She's safe. But I can't get this wound bound up until you get control of yourself. Come on, Mark. Remember who you are." Carl took a step forward, but the animal reared up, obviously pissed at that. Carl stopped, his hands up in the air. And when the bear growled, low in his throat, Carl took a step back. "Okay, okay. I get it. She's yours. But you're scaring her."

Julie wanted to snap that she sure as hell was not some bear's, but thought better of it. Especially as the animal dropped down to all fours to face Carl, not her.

Was it going to run away? Or attack Carl? Why the hell hadn't the idiot man run away when he had the chance? It wasn't like there were any more rocks up in this tree to throw at the creature. Fortunately, the thing didn't seem to be attacking anyway. It had just dropped down to stare at Carl, who took another slow step back.

"That's right, Mark. Remember who you are."

The bear released a long howl that was almost plaintive. And Julie had the weird thought that the two were really talking to each other. Carl and the bear in some bizarre conversation.

"Don't give me that shit, Mark. I'm your alpha, and I say face me as a *man*." The last word had the vibration of a command. Even Julie felt the power of it, though how a bear was going to understand that, she hadn't a clue.

Meanwhile, she heard the siren stop, and two car doors slammed. Both man and beast turned to the sound, but Carl bellowed first.

"Stay back! Don't shoot!"

A woman officer with short blond hair came tearing around the corner, but she pulled up short at the command. Her partner appeared next, a lanky guy who looked too young to be holding a gun.

"Oh, shit," the guy said, though it was more like a babble.

The woman held him back by putting a hand on his chest, but both of their eyes were on the bear.

"You're hurt, Carl, and he's out of control," the woman said.

"Stay out of it, Tonya," Carl growled. Lord, he was sounding more like a bear every second.

The woman glared, then slowly took a step forward, drawing her pistol as she moved. "Let me do this for you."

"Don't you fucking dare."

The woman stopped, and she gestured for her partner to stay back. But she didn't put away her gun. "Stevie," she said, her voice calm, "go get the tranq gun, will you?"

Her partner blanched. "What?"

"Go, slowly. Now."

The kid nodded, then backed away. One step. Two. Three. Then, at the edge of the house, he pivoted and ran. Which is when the woman spoke again.

"Okay, Mark. You've got about ten seconds until Stevie gets back. Carl's bleeding, and you're keeping me from helping him. Your alpha is hurt, and you're in the way. So you fucking switch back now, or so help me God—"

The bear moved. No, not so much moved as shimmered. Like a heat wave going through the air, creating a distortion or mirage. Julie was staring right at him when it happened, and she still could not process what she saw. The creature was on all fours when it started…doing whatever it was. One second she saw a huge black grizzly bear. The next, it seemed to shrink in on itself. The nose grew shorter, the hump lost fur. Then she saw skin, rippling with power or pain. She wasn't sure.

Then she saw legs and arms. The hard points of two shoulder blades before a man collapsed downward upon himself. He dropped and curled onto his side as he went. His head was tucked down, buried into forearms that came up and covered his face. But even so, she recognized him. Even lying dirty and howling on the ground, she knew who it was.

Mark.

She screamed.

Chapter 9

Mark transitioned back to a man for the stupidest of reasons. He needed to vomit. He'd learned young to not fight it. There were things that a bear ate that a man just didn't want in his belly. So within seconds of feeling cold sweat on bare skin, he struggled to his paws—hands—and purged with all the violence that entails.

And when he was done, he crouched in the grass and centered himself to the world around him. He found Julie immediately, hearing her tight whimpers of panic and smelling her terror like a dank miasma.

He'd done that to her. She was terrified of him.

Unable to deal with that, he allowed his senses to wander elsewhere. The birds weren't chirping, which might have been ominous except that Tonya and Carl were bickering a few feet away like angry children.

"I told you I'm fucking fine."

"And I told you that you've been sliced to hell by God only knows what that thing is, so you're going to the hospital where they're going to douse you in rubbing alcohol and antibiotics."

"Would you just back the hell off?"

"Would you rather I call your fiancée? She'll put you on bread and water for a week."

Fiancée? Carl had finally proposed? About damned time.

"Leave Becca out of it. And when did you start fighting dirty?"

"The minute you became alpha and thought that made you invincible." And then abruptly her tone shifted, becoming more professional as she turned to the newest scent, just coming around the corner. "Thanks for the blanket, Stevie. Go ahead and drop it around Mark's shoulders."

"I still don't understand where he came from," the young police officer said. "And where the bear went."

Oh, yeah. Stevie was a transfer from Virginia. He wasn't clued in on the whole bear-shifter thing. Which meant that Mark had to help cover until someone decided to bring the guy into the fold. So he sat back on his heels and rubbed at his mouth. "I was camping nearby," he lied. "Came when I heard the shots."

"Naked and unarmed?" Stevie drawled. "Dude, what did you think you could do?"

A blanket settled around his shoulders and—even better—a bottle of water appeared before him. He took both gratefully, rinsing and spitting before he ventured to speak. "Wasn't thinking. Wasn't fully awake until it was too late for me to change my mind."

Stevie chuckled, though he could tell by the sound it was more a way to relieve tension than true humor. Then the man turned toward the back property line. "How are you doing, Miss Simon? I brought a bottle for you, too."

"I saw…He—"

Tonya interrupted in her professional tone, quick to stop Julie from talking about what exactly she'd seen. "Feeling a little better, now? I know you probably have all sorts of questions. We certainly do. But it's better for everyone if you settle down a bit first. Drink that water and then we'll talk."

Stevie shifted his footing awkwardly in the grass, obviously confused by this. "But, Tonya—"

"Trust me on this," she snapped at her partner. "We've got our own way of doing things here."

"By stopping witness statements?" Stevie pushed. Obviously, the newbie wasn't a man to just ignore common sense. Good for him. But Tonya couldn't just drop the whole shifter thing on him, either, so she shut him down cold.

"You haven't even made it through your probationary period, Officer Harrison. You still need time to understand all of Gladwin's ins and outs."

"I don't—"

"Go check on the ME, will you? And help him carry all his crap here. We've got bodies we need to get under wraps. And one living man who needs an ambulance."

Carl growled under his breath, but didn't argue. Smart man. He wasn't going to win that particular argument. And as Stevie stomped toward the front of the property, Mark judged it high time to come back to the human world.

He slowly pushed to his feet, tightening the blanket around him. He didn't want to look directly at Julie, yet. Dreaded seeing the terror in her eyes. So he kept his head lowered until he faced at Carl.

"Jesus, you look like crap," he said.

Carl sat on the ground with Tonya standing protectively over him. The alpha looked haggard, and his shirt was a bloody rag. But the clean pad he pressed to his side was barely red. Which meant the worst of the bleeding was over. Carl had been looking over at the nearest body, eyes narrowed with worry, but at Mark's words, his gaze cut angrily back.

"I look like shit?" Carl said, his tone heavy with irony. "Maybe that's because my best friend is trying to get me to kill him."

Mark shook his head. "You have got to stop torturing yourself. When it happens, it happens. You need to accept it. I certainly have."

As Maximus of the Gladwin bear-shifters, Carl had the responsibility to kill any feral, including Mark. As bad as it was for Mark to slowly feel, day after day, pieces of his sanity getting lost to the bear, it was ten times worse for the alpha who had to watch it happen to his friend. Who had to wait, gun at the ready, dreading the day he would have to put a bullet in Mark's brain.

"You really need to learn to fight as a man, Mark," Tonya suggested. "With a gun and a cell phone."

"I didn't have time to get them," he said. "*That* was attacking." Mark looked at the nearest remains and was again hit by that nauseating sense of *wrong*. From what he could tell—and smell—it was a half-shifted human-bear where none of the pieces worked well together. It was just wrong and he flinched away from it. Especially since it was a dismembered mess, and he knew that he was the one who'd done the dismembering.

If he wasn't going to look there or at Carl, there was only one last place for his gaze to go. To Julie, with her horrified brown eyes and her tight swallows as she choked down both water and her fear. He'd been excruciatingly aware of her every moment that he'd been back as a functioning man. Hell, his bear had been focused on her, too, so he might as well face her now and the in-evitable destruction of his heart.

He took his time, though, studying her cuts and bruises long before meeting her gaze. She wasn't badly hurt, though there were tons of scrapes and she'd probably feel achy for days. He wanted to lick every wound clean and kiss the worry from her. Not going to happen, he knew, but he could wish for a miracle, couldn't he?

Her face was still pale, her brown eyes shone with tears. She was trying to come to grips with what she'd seen and was bal-anced on the knife's edge of rejecting everything to declare it a toxin-induced hallucination. Swamp gas or something. Nor-mals were known to come up with the weirdest explanations for shifters. But he didn't want her to be one of those blatant deniers—someone who would stubbornly fight the input of their own senses rather than face reality. So he smiled at her and—without clearing it with his alpha first—just flat-out told her the truth.

"Yes, Julie, everything you saw is real. I'm a shape-shifter. I change from man into bear and back again. When those things attacked, I protected you the best way I knew how: as a grizzly. I'm sorry I frightened you. I'm sorry you had to find out this way. But it's real and you're not crazy."

She looked at him, her eyes widening to an impossible size, but there was no other reaction to his words. Mark waited in anxious silence, as did Carl and Tonya, waiting to see what route she'd choose. Denial, hysteria, fainting spell? Or maybe she'd be okay with it. Maybe she'd accept it as easily as she might turn on the Syfy channel and drop into one of their mysterious worlds.

She didn't seem to do any of that. Her gaze—like his had a moment before—shifted to the nearby body parts. So he answered her questions before she could voice them.

"Those aren't normal, and they're not right. We don't know what they are, and I know they kind of looked like a bear, but they're not what I am. What..." He almost said, *What Carl and Tonya are,* but that wasn't his secret to tell. "What a lot of people are. There are werewolves, were-cats, were...whatevers. You can't catch it by a bite, and we don't go howling at the moon—"

"The dogs do," Tonya inserted with her typical dry humor.

Mark shot her an annoyed glare, but then immediately returned to Julie. "*We* don't, and I certainly don't. If you're trying to make logical, scientific sense of this, give it up. We've been working on that for generations. It's magic. Simple, unfathomable magic."

Julie choked, the sound half gasp, half sob. He went for her immediately, but she flinched back and he froze. She didn't even look at him, but stared at Carl. "Did I hit my head?" she asked.

"No," the alpha said gently. "It really happened. You're not crazy."

She stared, her body starkly rigid. It was the stance of a woman trying not to vomit.

"You're in shock right now," Mark said gently, hating the way her shoulder hunched when he spoke. "Give it some time. It's not a scary as it seems. Some people might even think it's fun. You know, like Hogwarts fun."

She took a couple deep breaths, both loud and unsteady. But then she knotted her hand into a fist and stared at the tree line. "Hogwarts? That's Harry Potter, right? Or was that a *Twilight* reference?"

Mark gaped at her. He knew what she was doing. Focus on trivialities rather than deal with the big shit. But seriously, who didn't know the difference between Harry Potter and *Twilight*? "Damn, do I have a movie list for you," he growled.

"Nah," Tonya inserted. "Read the books. Way better."

He would have said a lot more except the wail of a siren cut through their conversation. It was the ambulance, coming for Carl.

"Look, I know this is coming at you pretty fast," Carl said.

"Ya think?" Julie answered with her first show of temper since the danger had passed. Mark counted that as a good thing.

Then Carl cut in. "Normally, we reveal ourselves in a more controlled manner." He shot Mark a glare, but Mark just shrugged. So he broke protocol. What was Carl going to do? Shoot him? "We need you to not talk about this just yet. There are a lot of people who don't know."

"Like Stevie," Tonya said.

"And the ME," Mark added. Damned if he knew how they were going to get around the woman now.

Carl shook his head. "No, I brought her in when we found Theo. Had to."

Oh, right. And completely off point.

"In short," Tonya cut in, her gaze cutting to the front where Stevie was running around the corner with two paramedics in tow, "we'd really like you to confine your freak-out to us. For now."

Julie shot the woman a glare. "Do I look like I'm freaking out?"

"Yes, you do," Tonya said. "Though in a quiet way, which I really appreciate."

Julie looked at them one by one, ending with Mark. "On a scale from one to ten, I'm about twenty-seven on the freak-out scale. I start screaming at twenty-eight, so don't push it." Then she paused, and her body tightened as if bracing herself. "Any other surprises in store for me?"

"A ton, actually," Mark said and both Carl and Tonya shot him a glare. "But the worst is over. The rest will come once your logical mind comes back on line. It'll have doubts and questions and whatnot, but that's all perfectly normal." He shrugged. "At least as normal as this thing gets."

She looked at him then, holding his gaze while her eyes seemed to fill with all sorts of things he couldn't read. But she didn't speak because the paramedics had finally made it around the scattered body parts to start futzing with Carl.

Mark refused help. That was his norm. Nothing any doctor could do to help him. But he did stand around trying not to hover as they checked out Julie. She was good, but it was reassuring to hear them say it. As for Carl, his shifter healing had kicked in to stop the blood loss, but he still needed stitches. Not to mention a gallon of hydrogen peroxide.

Tonya had to go to the hospital with Carl. That was her job as beta to his alpha. She covered by claiming she'd take his statement. Stevie tried to grasp the opportunity to interview Julie, but Mark forestalled him.

"Tonya already took our statements. We can come by later to give more detailed information if you like, but for now, she's been through enough."

Stevie didn't like it, but it was hard for anyone to fight Mark when he used his don't-mess-with-the-dying-bear gaze. It was cold, hard, and filled with the subliminal threat to tear the guy limb from limb if he got annoying. The poor newbie caved, though it took him an impressive amount of time to give in.

So Mark turned to Julie as if he were going to escort her back to her house. Even a grizzly could be chivalrous, right? But she was already halfway up the backyard, her face carefully turned away from the body beside her back door.

"Oh, shit," he mumbled, then jogged to her side. Only, once there, he wasn't exactly sure what to do. He settled for a lame, "I'm so sorry, Julie—"

She held up her hand. They'd made it inside her house, but he was still a couple steps behind her. He desperately wanted to touch her, but her muscles were rigid, and her shoulders hunched. The body's way of screaming *Back off!* even if she was too polite to say it out loud.

He released a sigh. How quickly they'd fallen from where they'd started this morning. Pointless to pretend it didn't gouge a deep hole in his chest. Dying men didn't have the luxury of denying their feelings.

"I...I guess I'll just grab my clothes and go home," he said. Then he looked at his filthy hands. "Though, maybe I could take a shower first? If you don't mind?"

He could run home filthy. It wouldn't be the first time, but he was hoping to delay their separation. Maybe if she got a little time to process things, he could talk to her after he was fully clean. After he looked and smelled like a man instead of a beast. Maybe.

"Uh, sure," she said, her voice quiet. "Go on upstairs."

"I won't take long," he said, easing around her. Maybe if he could catch her eye. Maybe if she would look at him, things would be okay. But she stepped away from him into her father's office.

"Take as long as you like," she said, keeping her back to him.

He waited a moment, hoping she would turn around. He wanted to grab her and force her to face him. He wanted to beg her to not shut him out. Everything would be okay if she just gave it a little time. If they talked it through like human beings.

Except he wasn't a normal human being and even people who had been raised inside the shifter community didn't want to date him. He was too volatile and too close to feral. Which meant he really ought to just go.

He didn't.

He went upstairs and dove into the shower. He scrubbed himself three times, making sure to clean away anything and everything he could. He didn't worry about her safety. There were scores of police handling the mess in the backyard. That meant he could linger a while in the bathroom just to give her a little more time to process what had happened. And while he scrubbed, he mentally went through a dozen different scenarios of how he might approach her.

Should he start with facts? Give her the history of shifters as they knew it? Or how about silence? He could sit and wait for her questions, then answer them as best he could. Maybe he should feed her? They hadn't had breakfast and it was already lunchtime. He could handle her core needs, starting with a honey-cream latte at his house. He could make her another steak or order a pizza if that's what she preferred. Whatever she wanted, he would be there for her.

Eventually, his skin was rubbed raw and he couldn't lie to himself anymore. He was delaying facing Julie because he had no idea what to say to her. But he wouldn't find any answers until they were face-to-face. So he stepped out of the cold shower and toweled off. He delayed a few seconds longer while he buried his nose in her towel. He gloried in her scent on the fabric and then he walked to her bed. The scent of sex was still thick here, and it nearly brought him to his knees thinking that it was all over so quickly.

Eventually, he dressed and went downstairs to find her. He tried to scent her, but she wasn't in the den and with so many people tromping through the house, it was hard to isolate her. Maybe she was outside?

Five minutes later, the ME shook her head as she zipped a body into a bag. "Sorry, Mark. Julie drove off twenty minutes ago. Something about seeing her father in the hospital."

Chapter 10

Julie was jumping out of her skin. She thought leaving Gladwin would settle her brain and her stomach. Not so much. Her mind had jumped around so much that she'd had trouble driving straight. Her stomach had rebelled at the first smell of coffee, and only a chamomile tea and a chocolate chip cookie had stayed down. The first because it truly was soothing. The second because, damn it, she was not going to throw up chocolate no matter what she'd seen this morning.

Eventually, she made it to the hospital, but far from helping, that only made everything worse. She could barely concentrate on what was going on. Her thoughts kept shoving their way in between her sister's words.

"An infection…"

I had sex with a were-bear.

"Not uncommon."

I had great sex with a creature that shouldn't exist.

"A few more days."

Mark is a grizzly bear.

"Nothing to worry about."

Magical creatures existed and they gave really good head. Or at least Mark had.

Oh my God, I'm losing it.

Normally, when she was freaking out, she called her sister and received a good talking to. The girl was a science geek and deep into her PhD research into some miracle plant that destabilized cellular structure. Sounded lethal to her, but what did she know? She was just a legal secretary. Either way, her geek sis would spout all sorts of science facts with absolute authority, secure in the knowledge that she was the smartest person in the family. Whatever the topic, science and Ellen had the answer.

Except the woman obviously didn't know about grizzly bear–shifters. Or werewolves. Or magic. And if Julie broke her promise to keep this secret, her sister would likely have her checked into the psych ward. So as soon as she got to the hospital, Julie kept her mouth shut by eating everything in sight.

Not the best choice, but for some reason, powdered vending machine doughnuts also managed to stay down.

"What the hell is wrong with you today?" her sister finally demanded. "I thought a day away would help you relax, but you're not hearing anything. And would you please sit down?"

They were in the corridor outside of her father's room. With all the medical equipment, there was only one seat inside at a time, right now being occupied by their mother. Which left Julie pacing while her sister leaned against the sliding glass partition and glared at her.

"I heard every word you said," Julie lied. "Cell wall, blah blah blah. Telomeres, science stuff, science stuff."

"DNA strands," her sister ground out.

"Science sh—" Julie almost cursed, but belatedly remembered to moderate her language. Her mother had the sharpest ears and hated crudity in any form. Wonder what she'd say about a daughter who didn't say "shit" but had allowed a bear to lick her into a mind-blowing orgasm.

"Julie Ann!" her sister snapped, shifting into her most pompous tone. "Tell me what is going on this second or so help me God—"

"You'll what?" Julie said, rounding on her sister. "You'll tell Mom that I didn't listen to you blather about your research? You'll say I'm pacing and stuffing my face? Like any of that is new!"

Ellen's expression tightened into hurt, immediately making Julie feel guilty. "I'm trying to help here. What's going on?"

"It's nothing. I'm anxious about Dad."

"Bull. You weren't this insane when he was in surgery. It's just a minor fever. Dad will be fine." She leveled her with a hard stare. "So what's really going on?"

Well hell, give her sister points for being observant. "It's no big deal, okay? I've got it under control." How was that for a big, fat lie? Her sister didn't even bother arguing. She just reached over and grabbed the last doughnut, popping it into her mouth before Julie could take it back.

"Quit hiding behind food," Ellen said between dainty bites while powdered sugar floated to the floor around them.

Julie glared at her sister, killed a few more seconds by throwing out the empty doughnut box, then she shrugged. "Don't tell Dad, but there was an attack at the cabin."

"An attack? Like bears or something?"

Good thing she'd stopped eating because Julie would have choked at that. Instead, she managed a weak, "Or something. The police think it was burglary. Dad's tablet is gone and his computer has been messed with."

"What was it? A burglary or an attack?"

"I— Both. Burglary first. Attack second. I…uh…I came here rather than watch the ME deal with the bodies."

"*Bodies?*" The word came out as a high-pitched squeak that drew the attention of at least one steely-eyed nurse.

Julie nodded. "Three. Or maybe four. I don't know. It all happened so fast."

Ellen grabbed for the nearest chair and dropped down into it. "What happened?"

"I don't really know. Gunshots. Dead bodies. Me, screaming."

"Holy shit."

"Yeah. Mega holy shit." So much for watching their language. "I'm still really freaked. I'll have to go back and give a statement and stuff. It's actually lucky Dad can't go home just yet. I…Ellen, it was terrifying. Real blood isn't anything like TV blood."

"What exactly happened?"

Julie started to speak. It was on the tip of her tongue to tell her sister everything. Were-grizzlies. Things with muzzles and fur shooting at her. But instead, entirely different words came out of her mouth. "I don't want to think about it again."

"But—"

"I was upstairs. Bang bang. Dead people. Cops everywhere." There was so much more than that, but the words just wouldn't come.

"At Dad's cabin?"

She nodded. "All in the backyard."

"But how did the cops know to be there?"

"You remember Mark Robertson?"

Her sister frowned as she licked the powdered sugar off her fingers. "The summer hottie, star linebacker that looked like he could go NFL? Yeah, I vaguely remember fantasizing about him every night for a decade."

Ellen hadn't spent as much time at Dad's cabin as Julie had, but apparently her few weekends there had left an impression.

"Well, he…um…we kinda connected. And he was staying."

Her sister quickly muffled her squeal of surprise behind both her hands. But her eyes said a lot more as they danced in delight.

"Stop it," Julie said, her voice low.

Ellen peeled her hands down and whispered. "Spending the night as in on the couch? Or—"

"On the front porch."

Her sister's shoulders dropped. "Oh."

"It was this morning in the bed."

"Oh, yummy!" She leaned forward. "Well, if it couldn't have

been me jumping his bones, I'm glad it was you. So tell me the truth, was it good?"

Julie felt her face heat. "It was great. Right up until—you know."

"Oh, yuck. How awful. Did you at least get to the good part? Or was it all interrupted?"

"Afterglow was really short."

Her sister squeaked, this time an abbreviated giggle of delight. "Awesome?"

"Beyond awesome. And he's the one who heard the noise. He rushed out to…" Julie's insides softened at the memory. "He ran out to protect me."

"Ooooh. Protecting his woman, huh?"

Julie nodded. "You have no idea."

"Oh, God, I'd like to."

"No. No, no, no. After that it was awful and horrible and…" *Bizarrely magical.* Julie shuddered, the words caught in her throat.

"Wow, no wonder you're jumpy."

"It's not just that," she said, surprising herself with her words. "I don't know what to do about this. I mean, I live in Chicago. He's in Gladwin. And he's got…issues."

Ellen rolled her eyes. "Who doesn't? Look, you're worried about the wrong things here. With Dad sick, everything's in upheaval. So why not blow off steam with the hottie from high school?"

"I usually just ride my bike."

"Well, now you can ride him."

Julie huffed out a breath, wishing she could explain that sex with Mark wasn't the usual kind of sex. Well, it was, but he wasn't the usual kind of guy. In any respect. And her brain just couldn't process any of it. Bear-shifters? So ridiculously not possible. And yet it was true. Meanwhile, her sister grabbed her hand.

"Look, you've got reason to be freaked, but don't link him with the…crime thing. Did you have a good time with him?"

Julie nodded. "It was great." Right up until he changed into a freaking bear.

"Then don't look further than that. Not everything is about long-term thinking or life plans."

"Says the woman in a seven-year PhD program."

"Which means I know exactly what I'm doing long term and what is an of-the-moment kind of thing. Hottie from summer loving? Of the moment. Promotion at the law firm? Long term. Don't make it any more complicated than that."

Good advice, but it didn't even begin to address the whole magical creatures thing. Julie took a deep breath—in and out—as she tried to work out exactly what to say. As usual, her sister didn't give her the chance to talk.

"Julie, you gotta go back there."

"What?"

"First off, you're not worth a damn right now. You're too freaked. Second, you can't hide it. Mom will notice the minute she steps out for coffee. Dad will be on it eventually because even he isn't that blind."

"You sure?"

"I'm sure. The first thing he'll ask is about his research. Then you'll have to tell him—"

"Why I couldn't find his tablet, blah blah blah."

"And the whole thing will come out." She paused to wink at her sister. "No pun intended."

"Ew!"

"Last—and this is most important—you've been without a date for how many years now? Don't mention how long since Dickwad."

"Stop it. His name was—"

"I don't care. He was a jerk. You deserve better."

She sighed, wishing she had more doughnuts at hand. "I'm not going back there to get laid."

"No, you're not," Ellen said sternly. "You're going back there to receive delivery of the hospital bed and stock the kitchen. Plus bleach the entire damned house because you know Dad hasn't done that since ever. And if by chance, you happen to run into Mark, then that is purely coincidence. And I hope you two *coincidence* like rabbits until Dad gets there."

Julie looked away, her gut twisting high in her throat. "It's not that easy."

Ellen stood and gently wrapped her sister in her arms. "It never has been, at least not for you. But that's okay. Take the fun while you can. It's going to be hard enough to keep your sanity when Dad gets there."

Well, that was certainly true. Meanwhile, another voice interrupted their discussion. It was their mother, her voice sounding tried and strained.

"Don't worry, honey. Your dad is going to be fine."

Julie separated from her sister and reached out to give her mother a kiss. "I know. We were just having a moment of sister bonding, that's all."

"Guess what?" Ellen said, her voice suspiciously perky. "Julie just agreed to go back to the cabin and clean it up for Dad. She's going to stay with him while he recuperates."

Her mother's eyes narrowed with concern. "Are you sure? Can you take that much time off from work?"

"She took two weeks," Ellen answered before Julie could. "And I have to get back to the lab. You're doing great, but we both know you're barely keeping yourself from strangling the man as it is."

Julie's mom nodded her agreement. Their divorce had been the best thing for both of them. A week in the same cabin would have them at each other's throats. So that left Julie as nursemaid.

"Are you sure, honey?"

"Yes," she finally said. It made sense even if that meant she had to face the whole Mark issue. Magic and all. "I'll go back tonight. I just have to ask Dad a few question about his research."

"Well, he's awake. Best to do it now before he gets too tired. Though be prepared for an earful."

Didn't she know it? One question about his research and her father could talk the ears off a bushel of corn. But Julie was counting on that. She wanted to know exactly what kind of fairy tale her father had been working on. All she knew was that they were particular to the Gladwin area. Was it possible that he knew about shifters, too? If so, then they had a lot to talk about. But only if her mom and Ellen weren't around.

"How about you two go out for lunch? I'll hang with Dad for a while here."

Her mother gave her a grateful hug. "Thanks, honey."

Her sister, on the other hand, gave her a lascivious grin. "Make sure you get back to Gladwin well before dark. You should plan on eating dinner at that café where everyone goes. Who knows who you might hook up with while you're there?"

Julie shot her sister a glare, but Ellen just waggled her eyebrows at her. Then the two were gone, leaving Julie to find a delicate way to ask her father if he believed in magical were-bears.

* * *

A couple hours later, Julie was back in Gladwin and wondering exactly who was in on the secret and who wasn't. Unable to face her father's cabin, she headed instead to the Lucky Latte Café. Ten years ago, it had been Lucky Lucy's Diner, but the newest owner put in an espresso machine and changed the name to grab onto the yuppie coffee craze. It worked. And since the menu also included burgers and onion rings, Julie was all too happy to settle down to some greasy delight.

Except five minutes after being shown to a booth, Julie began to realize that something significant had changed while she was away.

People knew her. People she'd never met greeted her by name. They smiled at her and patted her shoulder as they passed by.

They waved from across the room before sitting down to their meals. And then, a too-perky blonde dropped into the opposite side of the booth and pushed a cupcake toward her. It was mega large and decorated with a grizzly bear face, complete with chocolate drops for eyes and a long icing nose.

"You're Julie Simon, right? I'm Becca, Carl's fiancée." Then she gestured to the cupcake. "What do you think? Too on the nose?"

"What?" Julie said.

"On the nose. It means too obvious. Too on point. Too—"

"I know what it means," Julie interrupted, not upset. More confused and off-kilter. "Why are you asking me?"

"I'm a baker. I have a store in Kalamazoo, but I'm setting one up here, too. So I thought, what better way to welcome you to the fold than to give you a grizzly bear cupcake?" She grinned, and Julie had to admit that the look was infectious. The woman seemed to be just naturally perky, which was endearing. A little annoying, but generally endearing.

"Uh. Thanks." What else was she supposed to say? *I don't want to be part of your freaky magic cult? I don't like suddenly knowing something I can't share with anyone else and makes my father treat me like a six-year-old?* Yeah, she'd been stupid enough to broach the topic with her father. Could real shifters exist? Maybe? He'd laughed in that condescending way men have when looking at a silly woman. "I thought you'd grown out of your fanciful childhood," he'd said. And when she'd stiffened, he'd patted her hand. "You're a good girl," he'd said and then his eyes had drifted closed.

So much for hoping her father was aware of the truth. But looking around at the friendly faces in the café, she realized she wasn't completely alone. All of them were part of the secret. And they were welcoming her into the tribe, so to speak. "Is everyone here a…Do they all…?" She cut off her words, struggling to find a way to ask what she wasn't supposed to talk about. What she could barely bring herself to comprehend.

"Part of the Gladwin grizzly clan?" Becca asked cheerfully. She looked around at the crowd, about twenty strong. "About half," she finally said. "Big events bring people out for gossip. And this morning was a big event."

Julie looked away. In her mind there were two big events. The first was the hot morning with Mark. The second was…well, the violent, awful morning with grizzly bear Mark.

"Too soon, huh?" Becca asked, her voice sympathetic. "I can relate. I was, um, brought into the fold in less-than-ideal circumstances."

Julie's gaze jumped back to her. "What happened?"

"My adopted son was kidnapped. Long story, but with a happy ending." She flashed Julie a quick smile. "Look, you're probably freaked out right now."

"Ya think?"

"But it gets better. I promise. And we're all really happy that you and Mark have found each other."

Julie took a moment to process what she'd heard. And another moment to make sure the words meant what she thought they did. "Mark and I…Do you think that we…" She looked around the room. There were no less than three people beaming smiles at her that very second. "I knew small towns had a good rumor mill, but this is ridiculous."

Becca frowned as she looked down at the cupcake. "Okay, maybe I'm off here, but Tonya said you know about…um…"

"That Mark can stand up really tall and furry? Yeah. I know that."

"And Carl told me that the two of you were together."

"At the time of the attack? Yes, he was there with me."

"Er, right." Becca shifted uncomfortably in her seat. "The thing is, bears can smell really well. They can scent—"

"Oh, shit." Now it was her turn to flush bright pink. So everyone here knew that she and Mark had made love. Great.

Becca touched her hand. "We think it's great."

"Except it's not great," Julie snapped. "It's not anything at all. I'm here for a week to help my dad. And even if there was something…there isn't."

"Because of the bear thing?"

Well, yeah. Plus the fact that before yesterday, they hadn't seen each other in years. "Look, it's not the 1800s. Sometimes single adults hook up. Don't make more of this than it is."

"Okay. Sure. But you should know that Mark doesn't."

"What?"

"Mark doesn't hook up. He's the most reclusive guy I've ever known. He barely speaks, rarely comes out of his den, and when he does, it's to be surly." She shrugged self-consciously as if suddenly realizing what she'd said. "No offense."

Julie thought back to the first hour with Mark the day before. "None taken. 'Surly' is a nice word for how he wakes."

Becca flashed her a quick smile. "Like a bear with a sore paw?"

Julie nearly choked on her soda. Fortunately, her cheeseburger arrived. The waitress set it down with a thump. "On the house," the woman said with a toothy grin. "Welcome to the community."

"Oh, hell no," Julie said, startling everyone. But Julie didn't stop. She turned to the room at large, stunned that she was doing this. She couldn't imagine this scene in Chicago where most people didn't even recognize their neighbor much less care whom they slept with. "Sorry, everyone. Mark and I aren't dating. We're not going steady, getting pinned or..." She couldn't think of any more terms from the 1950s. "We're just not, okay? I'm here to help my dad, then I'm going back to my life in Chicago."

Half the room looked at her like she'd lost her mind. The other half glared at her like she'd just betrayed one of their favorite sons. And not a one of them said a single thing. At least not to her. After about ten extremely awkward seconds, they pointedly turned their backs to her. They spoke in low murmurs to each other or silently ate their food. And not a one of them gave her another smile.

Julie looked down at her food, feeling completely mortified. But that only brought her gaze to the cupcake and the über-friendly grizzly face on top. With a sigh, she pushed it back toward Becca. "You should probably eat this."

Becca picked it up and peeled off the wrapping. "How about we split it?"

Julie stared at the beautiful confection, her mouth watering at what had to be a killer amount of calories. And yet, it really looked delicious. "Sure."

"And don't worry about what everyone else thinks. We all just want a happy ending for Mark, you know?"

No, she didn't know. *What the hell— Oh, right.* In all the bizarre happenings of this morning, she'd completely forgotten about what started the whole kissing thing this morning. Mark had told her he was dying. And how the hell had that slipped her mind?

She stared at her food, unable to move. And now the sight of Becca cutting that cute bear face in half chilled her down to her bones. "Do all…Do they all die young?" God, the idea was horrifying.

"What? Oh, no. Just the…um…really unlucky ones."

Mark. She slumped back in her seat and rubbed her hand over her face. "I don't understand any of this."

"No reason you should," a cold voice said over her shoulder. Julie spun around to see the female officer from this morning. Her tag read "Kappes."

Meanwhile, Becca sighed. "Hello, Tonya."

"Hello, Mrs. Max," the woman returned without much warmth. Clearly, there wasn't a whole lot of love between these two. Meanwhile, Officer Kappes turned to Julie. "Glad to see you back here. I was worried when you took off this morning."

"My dad's in the hospital. I had to go see him."

"So I understand. But I'd really like to talk to you about this morning."

"Can't right now," Julie said as she grabbed her cheeseburger. "I'm eating."

The woman showed her teeth and slid right into the booth beside Becca. "No problem. We'll have girl talk while I wait."

Becca rolled her eyes. "Like you girl talk."

"Hey!" the officer said, sounding insulted. "I have girly parts. I talk."

"Not the same thing."

Definitely not. She couldn't imagine this officer as anything but prickly, cold, and…and hell, now she remembered Tonya Kappes from summers in Gladwin. She'd been a tall tomboy with no time for Becca. And once during Becca's first summer here, Tonya had dressed slutty and made out with Carl's younger brother Alan at a birthday party. The gossip had been loud enough that even Becca had heard it.

But that was years ago, and the woman had obviously grown up to be all business. Which was exactly what Julie had been wishing for just a moment ago. She hadn't wanted all the small-town gossips poking their noses into her love life. And so like an answer to her prayers, in comes a woman who could give Joe Friday a run for his money. She practically embodied, "Just the facts, ma'am." Which meant that if anyone could give her straight answers, it was Officer Kappes.

Thinking hard, Julie swallowed down a bite of pretty amazing burger and grabbed an onion ring. The other two women had degenerated into small talk. *How's the new bakery coming? Fine. How's the keeping-the-peace business? Not so peaceful.* And while those words were being exchanged, Julie came to a decision.

When the small talk eased, she gestured to the sliced-in-half bear cupcake. "Obviously, you know about the bears? Are you one of them?"

Becca shook her head, but the officer nodded.

"Became furry with my first period."

Julie winced. That certainly painted a picture. But come to think of it, this was just the type of information she needed. Simple facts, uncomfortably graphic. "Okay. I need answers."

"So do I. Need to know why those things attacked you."

"Haven't a clue. Why is Mark dying?"

"He's not dying. He's just becoming furry way too much. Eventually he won't be able to go back."

Oh. Well, that sucked. "But, um, he'll live out a natural life then? As a—"

"Not likely. Someone who can't go back tends to go crazy. Someone will have to put him down."

Julie stared at the officer in shock. "That's murder."

"Ever seen an enraged grizzly? One that is out of control? It destroys everything around it. It roars like it's in pain, probably is because it's using teeth and claws to tear everything apart. Buildings, cars, people. The paws get torn to shreds, the muzzle is next. But even after that, it's still hundreds of pounds of bone and muscle lumbering around like Godzilla. It'll snatch up a person like a doll and squeeze until the ribcage pops."

"Tonya!" Becca hissed. "There are children here."

Julie belatedly realized that while she'd been gaping in horror, the rest of the café had been listening in. The whole place was silent, and when Julie looked around, people dropped their gazes to their food. No one was eating anymore.

Then the waitress piped in, her voice loud in the awkward silence. "Always a pleasure having you visit us, Tonya. Do let me fix you an order *to go*."

The officer looked up, her cheeks stained a dull red. "Uh, yeah. Sorry, Robin."

Then Becca spoke up, her gaze on Julie, but her voice pitched to everyone around them. "But there's lots of hope, too. There's your father's research, for one. That's why we're all so glad he's feeling better. When's he coming home, Julie?"

Julie frowned. Her father's research? What did fairy tales have to do with this? "Um, a few days."

"That's great. So are you here to get things set at the cabin?"

"Uh, yeah. What about Dad's research?"

Becca popped a bite of cupcake into her mouth. "Well, Carl said that there was some promising stuff in the old stories. That's why he asked everyone to help your dad collect them. You know, tell him whatever Great-Grandpa Jones ever said about anything."

"Promising—"

"You want me to box that up for you?" interrupted waitress Robin as she held out a Styrofoam box. "I'm sure you've got lots of things to do. Market down the street is having a sale on hot dog buns. I swear your father lived on hot dogs and my burgers." Then her expression softened. "Also got all sorts of beer and wine, too. Just in case."

Julie bit her lip, her mind whirling. Thoughts jumbled around in her brain, but they all landed with the two women across from her. They had information she wanted. It wasn't just the history of shifters, but answers about Mark and what happened this morning. These were questions she wasn't ready to ask Mark, but she could ask these two. Especially if there was a little extra lubricant with the discussion.

"Dad has a blender," she said. "And I sure as hell can't face that backyard without a margarita or three. Anyone care to join me?"

Chapter 11

Raucous female laughter crashed into Mark's ears as he got out of his truck. The first thing he did was extend his senses throughout the cabin property. He scented Julie, Becca, and Tonya, but also the dozens of other people who had milled about the property this morning. The lingering scent of those *wrong* things felt like an itch under his skin, and he bared his teeth at its presence so near Julie. But he kept his grizzly under wraps. For one thing, Carl had arrived a few minutes ago and was watching him closely from the front porch. For another, he didn't want to freak out Julie any more than she already was.

His nostrils twitched as another grizzly-shifter rounded the corner. It was one of the Gladwins, set to patrol the property. Carl signaled that guard duty was over. At least for the young bear. Mark would cover protection duty for the rest of the night. Him plus all the high-end electronics he'd had installed this afternoon. That was one of the advantages of being filthy rich and not having more than a few months to spend it. He could pay an exorbitant amount to have the surveillance equipment installed immediately. Especially since he wasn't opposed to a bit of bribery.

Another fit of giggles filled the air, and Mark raised an eyebrow at Carl. Was that Becca who'd just brayed like a donkey? Carl shrugged, his expression saying that he thought the sound adorable. Mark could relate. He was pretty sure he heard a few of Julie's indelicate snorts and couldn't help but grin. He'd been worried that she'd gone close to catatonic at the revelation of magic in the world. Instead, she handled it in a healthier manner. She'd gotten drunk with friends.

Then he heard Tonya hoot with laughter, the sound high pitched and girly. Lord, if she knew they were outside listening in, she'd shoot them for sure. That was not a sound the tough-as-nails Officer Kappes would ever make. Not sober, at least.

Mark stopped on the front porch, using his smart phone to check in on the electronics. Everything appeared quiet. Carl joined him soon afterward, his eyes narrowed as he scanned the phone.

"She'd still be safer at your place."

Maybe, but she'd never go. Not if this morning's freak-out was any indication. And more important, she wouldn't be safe. Not from him. Not if she wandered through his den, setting her body and her scent in the most intimate place of his life. No, then he'd bolt the doors and drag her caveman-style to his bed. It had been hard enough going into his kitchen and smelling her there. No way was he going to torture himself by having her in his living area.

Meanwhile, Carl took Mark's silence as the denial it was. He sighed and gestured to the road. "The cops are going to drive over once around midnight and again at five. They won't knock unless they see something wrong. Ron and Joe will be patrolling as grizzlies until—"

"I got it. It's covered. And I'll be here watching the monitors. Besides, I don't think there can be more of those things around anyway."

Carl's face tightened. "Except for the one that got away. You think it was the Crazy Cat Lady?"

Mark's bared his teeth. He couldn't stop himself when thinking about the bitch who'd abducted young shifters and who had certainly been part of the attackers this morning. If only he'd kept it together, he could have chased the bitch and ended this whole nightmare right then and there. Instead, the mating imperative had taken over. His grizzly brain had decided to stake his claim on Julie while simultaneously warning Carl away. In reality, he'd scared the shit out of her, chased her up a tree, and let the cat bitch escape. Not his finest moment.

"You saved her life today. Mine, too, so don't get caught up in your head."

"Better than trapped in my grizzly." The sentence came out more as a snarled growl, but at least they were words.

Carl didn't have a comeback to that, so he simply squeezed Mark's arm. "Stay human, okay?"

"Yes, Mother Hen," he said. But in his mind, he was repeat-

ing the words, *Stay human, stay sane.* The motto might as well
be tattooed on the back of his eyelids. Mark had barely made
it back from this morning's shift. He probably wouldn't be able
to the next time. So any hope of extra time with Julie meant
staying human. Not that she wanted to hang out with him either way, but a guy could hope. And these days, hope was all he
had.

They were just about to knock on the front door when a
haunting alto voice filled the air. It was Tonya, singing a lullaby in
rich notes that startled both men.

"Did you know she could sing?" Mark whispered.

Carl shook his head while they both listened to words that
they'd never heard before. It was "Hush Little Baby" done dif-
ferently. Instead of buying the child a mockingbird, Mama got
him a ruby-throated loon, a silver spoon, a quick-fingered witch,
then blood and a kiss. It was the oddest list of items he'd ever
heard—especially in a child's lullaby—but folk songs were not
something he'd ever paid any attention to.

The song ended and the ladies clapped enthusiastically.
Mark would have, too, except that he was sure it would em-
barrass Tonya. And then someone—probably Tonya—let out
a loud burp, causing gales of laughter. God, it was beautiful
to hear that. Joy. Silly conversation. Women in friendship. All
things he missed when he was a grizzly. This moment of eaves-
dropping became startlingly precious to him simply because he
wouldn't be able to appreciate it for much longer. And he was
both awed by the beauty of it and pissed off because he was
outside of it. Like God was busy shoving him out the door of

humanity just when he really began to see how special it was.

Angered by that, he slammed his fist against the door. The sound was loud, the impact enough to make his hand burn. And even worse, the laughter stopped as abruptly as a TV turning off. What a child he was, destroying the fun when he couldn't be a part of it.

Tonya opened the door, her face was flushed red, but her hand was steady where it gripped the pistol at her hip. Mark was surprised, but Carl stiffened in fury.

"You are not drunk and carrying a loaded pistol," he snapped.

She bit her lip, slowly pulling her hands into view. "Not carrying anything," she said.

Carl wasn't having any of it. He grabbed the weapon out of her belt with all the authority of an alpha. He double-checked the safety—on, thank God—and glared at his beta.

"We've got enough problems without you being stupid."

Tonya flushed and canted her gaze away. And then she jerked her short hair back as she extended the motion, baring her neck to Carl. "You're right," she said. "I hadn't expected to drink this much."

"At all, Tonya. Only an idiot carries a weapon *and* drinks."

She nodded, her throat still exposed. Behind her, Becca came forward clearly unsteady on her feet. "She only had one," Becca said. "I might have had four."

Mark suppressed a chuckle. With Becca's petite frame, four would make her totally sloshed.

"And I split the difference with two and a half," added Julie as she raised her glass. But once it came into view, she tipped it back to her mouth. A moment later, it was empty. "Three," she said with a satisfied smack of her lips.

Good lord, she was beautiful. Flushed cheeks, bright red lips, sparkling eyes, and a body that seemed to sway mesmerizingly before him. He'd gotten used to having the lust slam into him at the sight of her, but this time it was lust tinged with laughter. Hunger sweetened with delight.

"You better sit down," Mark said as he crossed to Julie's side, his nostrils flaring as he came close. Spicy citrus scent filled his mind, and he remembered just where she smelled juiciest. Without even willing it, he stroked her arm and drew her tight against him.

But instead of melting into him like he'd expected, she stiffened, pulling away with a sniff. She opened her mouth to say something, her hand coming up with a single finger extended toward him. He steeled his spine, waiting to hear her condemn him. Filthy animal. Ugly bear. Murdering monster. All of those words vibrated in his brain. All that remained was for her to pick which ones.

But she didn't say anything. She just pointed at him and held still. Then abruptly, she walked back over to the couch and dropped down hard enough to make the feet skid on the wood floor.

Becca chuckled. "That's telling him!"

Tonya nodded. "Very succinct."

Julie just rolled her eyes at them, which produced a choked-off laugh from Becca and a breathy exhale from Tonya.

"I think that's my cue to leave," Becca added, still chuckling.

Carl grabbed Tonya's arm with one hand and Becca's shoulder with the other. "Neither of you is driving."

"Well, duh," Becca said as she reached up on tiptoe to press a kiss to his jaw. "That's why you're here."

Carl blew out a breath. That was, in fact, why he was here. Meanwhile, Tonya pulled out her cell phone, clearly looking for messages. "Any news?" Her voice was as crisp as usual. And given how fast a shifter could metabolize alcohol, it was likely she was close to sober.

"Nothing new," Mark answered. Then he glanced at Julie, wondering exactly how much she'd been told or had guessed about this morning's attack. He was about to ask when Tonya thunked him on the back of the head. He whipped around to glare at her—or worse—only to be met with another pointed finger, this one Becca's.

"She's not stupid, and we like her."

"Definitely," Tonya added.

"So tell her the truth," Becca continued.

"I have," he growled. "I am." He'd been honest with her from the very beginning and was set to answer all the rest of her questions tonight.

"Not *that* truth," Becca said. And when he frowned, Tonya put up her hands like bear claws and growled. Becca giggled as she continued. "We told her about shifters." She pressed her hand flat on Mark's chest. "She needs *this* truth. The heart stuff."

His heart? He didn't have one anymore. Not for a few years now since he realized there was no hope left for him.

"Don't you look away from me," Becca snapped in her sharpest stern-mother voice. "There's still time."

Was there? He looked at Julie, who was watching everything with wide eyes. Watching, but not expressing. He had no idea what she was thinking and that made man and bear twitchy. "I'll tell you anything you want to know," he said to her.

Julie bit into her lower lip. "I don't know what to ask."

"So work it out!" ordered Becca. For a petite human, she was stepping fully into the role of Mrs. Max. Then she flashed them a beaming smile before stepping carefully out the front door. "And now we're leaving," she called, grabbing hold of Tonya as they headed toward Carl's truck. For his part, Carl was shaking his head even as he turned back to Mark.

"You okay here?"

"Quit being a mother hen."

"Quit shoving your head up your ass." Then Carl turned to Julie. "He's grumpy half the time, and too arrogant all of it. But he's a good man when he comes out of that cave of a house. Please give him a chance."

Jesus. Now he had his alpha trying to help his love life. Could anything be more humiliating? "If you don't leave this instant, I'm going to fuck up your Internet so bad—"

"Gotta go!" Carl said with a quick wave. "I'll come by in the morning."

"Come late. Like in a month." Mark nearly shoved the man out the door.

"Roger that," Carl said with a grin.

Neither of them had been in the military or police, but they'd both been using the term since they were eight and pretending to be part of a SWAT team. It was familiar and carried the echo of childhood games. And especially now with the end so near, it made Carl smile.

"Roger that," he echoed. Outside, Becca started singing a mangled version of "Jack the Knife" in a belting soprano. Inside, Mark balanced awkwardly on the balls of his feet. It was a predatory stance that meant his grizzly was already stalking Julie. Which was a really bad idea since he had no clue how to read her mood.

"They're nice people," Julie finally said, her gaze going to the window. "Once Tonya relaxes, she's nothing like her officer persona."

"Really? She's had a stick up her ass since middle school."

"Really," Julie said, her lips curving in a soft smile that made him want to kiss her for the rest of his life. "She's a lot softer on the inside than she lets on. Not surprising she's had to be tough. She's a woman police officer."

"And beta to Carl."

"Right. Which means she can't let her guard down anywhere."

Mark prowled across the room. He wanted to sit beside her on the couch, but instead, perched gingerly on the edge of her father's recliner. "She let it down with you." He doubted she knew the miracle that was.

"That's 'cause we don't count," Julie said, dismissing his compliment even before he got a chance to say it. "We're not part of the pack and we're certainly not police."

"Becca's Mrs. Max. She and Carl haven't gotten married yet,

but everyone knows they're mates. That makes her part of the pack. And you…" His voice trailed away. "What did you do to get her to sing?"

Julie shrugged. "I didn't do anything. I just talked to her." Then she quieted before looking oddly at him. "I listened."

"And she sang?"

"Yeah. I could tell that she wanted me to get comfortable with the whole bear thing. And I wanted to know the real her. So…" She gestured at an empty glass. "I made her margarita triple strength, dared her to drink it, and then started sharing stuff about my childhood."

He blinked. "Like what?"

"Doesn't matter. Embarrassing stuff. She had to reciprocate, so she sang."

Of course she did. Just like Mark had sung as well. Not literally, but certainly he'd spilled his guts to Julie more than he had to anyone else. They'd reconnected barely more than twenty-four hours ago, and yet by this morning, he'd confessed so much about his feelings for her. About his adolescent needs and the way their one night as teenagers still haunted him. He'd told her all that simply because she'd listened. And because she was Julie.

And while he mulled over that, Julie held up her phone with a grin.

"Plus, I never told her I was recording it."

Holy shit! "She'll probably shoot your phone when she finds out."

Julie grinned. "I won't tell. I like to keep my blackmail material secret until I really need it."

"Very wise," he said. Then he fell silent, as did she.

Ticks of the clock grew louder as he looked at her. Just this morning, so many things had felt possible. Now, he was stuck across the room from her, trying to figure out what he was supposed to do.

And while he dithered, Julie exhaled loudly, folded her arms across her chest, and pinned him with a heavy glare.

"So now that you've effectively killed my buzz, I figure it's time I kill yours."

Oh, shit. "Um, what?"

"You're going to tell me exactly what those things were this morning and what the hell they want with my father."

Oh, goody. Because it wasn't enough that she got introduced to the shifter world today. Now she insisted on finding out that there were honest-to-goodness sicko bastards in the magical realm, too.

Chapter 12

Julie watched Mark settle back in her father's recliner, looking like a man facing a firing squad.

"I don't know what they are or why they attacked," he said. "We have guesses, but nothing for certain."

"And they are?"

He huffed out a breath. "Complicated."

She matched him with her own heavy exhale. Julie had one goal this evening: to get answers. At least that's what her tequila-sloshed brain told her. Sadly, that goal seemed to be at odds with what her body wanted.

Her body was all about noticing that Mark had shaved and changed, which made him look kind of dashing. Especially since he'd put on dark jeans and a plain black tee that hugged every ripped inch of him. No tats. Clean nails. And eyes that looked straight at her even as he seemed to be apologizing without even opening his mouth.

Weird. What did he have to be sorry for? Saving her life? Giving her great head? Or maybe it was that other part. The part about being a freaking bear. And since she'd just consumed enough tequila to wash away the filter between her brain and her mouth, questions just spilled out.

"Are you ashamed of being a bear?"

"Grizzly," he corrected. "And no shame."

She narrowed her eyes, trying to gauge if he lied. Men were notoriously clueless about their own emotions, but there seemed to be no half measure in his answer. And when she looked at him—evenly shaved and neatly dressed—she could sense the animal just below the surface. It was in the way he moved, she thought, or didn't move. Right now, he sat with an animal stillness, a wary patience broken only by the occasional twitch of his nose. And when he moved, it was smooth and substantial. She'd assumed it was because he was a large man, but now she saw it as more. He carried the bear's weight even as a man. The sheer power of a large predator, raw and untamed.

"Are *you* ashamed?" he asked.

She frowned. "Ashamed? Of what?"

"Going to bed with me? Of letting me—"

"No," she said, cutting him off. The last thing her semi-drunk mind needed was a reminder of what they'd done this morning. Of how thoroughly he'd gotten her off and how much she really wanted to do that again.

"Repulsed, then," he said, not even expressing it as a question.

"No," she repeated more firmly. "I'm freaked, that's for sure."

But still thoroughly aroused. "I mean what if you'd…you know, changed right in the middle?"

He shook his head. "Doesn't happen."

"Really? Why not?"

"Don't know. I mean, sure, if it's two shifters—usually teenagers—they'll do it simultaneously. I think they feed off each other somehow. But the magic doesn't work when intimate with a human. I don't know why. And believe me, people have tried."

"Magic?" Not a word she could possibly use as simple fact. And yet, the way he spoke, it was like he completely believed in fairy dust and magic potions.

He arched a brow. "Yes, magic. Energy. Whatever word you want to use. Just the weight differential alone can't be explained by science. I'm a big guy, but I'm not carrying the five hundred pounds I do as a grizzly."

She would have guessed more, but that was because to her brain, huge was just huge. Five hundred or five thousand pounds made little difference when the creature was stretching up to face her in the tree. And now she sat across from the same creature, only he was a man and he looked uncomfortable perched on the edge of her dad's recliner.

"So you call it magic?"

"I do. It's an easy catchall phrase. Talk to the scientists if you want something more technical."

On her to-do list, though she doubted she'd understand it. She was not the science type. "And those things that attacked. They were shifters?"

He shook his head. "They were wrong people." He held up a

hand before she could question. "They smelled wrong, so that's what I've labeled them. It's like they were half shifted. A muzzle, some fur, weird eyes."

She hadn't noticed the eyes. She hadn't wanted to look that closely.

"Carl talked to the ME an hour ago. It's preliminary, but she thinks their animal DNA was triggered somehow. But they weren't natural-born shifters. They didn't have the full ability to change and so only parts of them did. It shouldn't be possible." His shoulders twitched and his face tightened in revulsion. "They were just *wrong*."

"But why would they come here? Why would they attack my father?"

Mark held up his hands. "I don't know. Maybe they want your father's research."

"But why? They're fairy tales."

"About shifters." He leaned forward onto his knees, but the gesture wasn't casual. Nothing about his movements ever was. "Think. You've just learned that magic is real. What would that mean about all those obscure local fairy tales that fascinate your father? What if they contain answers? Magic spells, incantations, stripping naked and braying at the moon. They're all in those stories, and we have no idea how much is truth and how much is fiction."

"But Dad just thinks they're silly."

"And yet he's spent the last decade studying them."

Her eyes narrowed. "I asked him point blank this afternoon. I said, 'What if people really could change shape?'"

"And wouldn't you deny it if you were him? If you suspected that magic was real and that shape-shifters walk around with us every day. You've just had a triple bypass, you've got a fever and are hospitalized. Last thing you want is to give anyone the idea that something's wrong with your brain."

She bit her lip. Okay, so that made sense. "We should tell him—"

"No!"

She recoiled backward from the force of his word. But a moment later, she felt her anger surging to the fore. "You'd let my father spend his life researching stuff and withhold the answer?"

"It's not the answer."

"It's part of it!"

His fingers turned white where he gripped his knees. That was it. The rest of him was still as if he held himself back by sheer willpower. "Will your father keep this secret?"

"Maybe it shouldn't be a secret!" The world was 180 degrees different from what she'd thought. From what just about everyone thought. Why weren't they shouting it from the rooftops? Why hadn't any of them gone onto CNN and just said, *Here you go. Magic is real.*

His eyes narrowed, and his words came out in a careful, measured tempo. "We've existed for thousands of years. Don't you think someone somewhere has talked?"

Um, yeah. Probably.

His hands lifted off his knees to pull tighter against his torso. Almost like he was forcing himself to keep from reaching out. "Magic doesn't want to be found."

She gaped at him. "Come again?"

"It's a weird mystery of life. Shifter history is filled with people who talked or normals who figured things out. But it ends badly. Witches burned at the stake, magicians convicted of unholy knowledge."

"Religious fanatics have always existed," she said. "But we're in the age of reason now."

He blew out a slow breath. "Science hasn't been so good at stopping ISIS or the religious right. They've only armed the nutcases with nukes."

She grimaced. "Okay, so you've got me there. But—"

"It's not just the fanatics," he interrupted. "There have been communities where it's an open secret. Something always goes wrong. Like Atlantis."

"The island that blew itself up sometime in prehistory?"

"That's the one. Pompeii and Camelot were others."

She snorted. "You're just making this up."

He sighed. "I wish I were. There are texts."

"What? Where?"

"Carl has some." He flashed her a weak smile. "Alphas have searched for this answer. It's their job to keep the clan safe. Many have revealed themselves." He growled low, the sound nearly inaudible. "Eventually it goes wrong."

Was this even possible? It didn't seem credible, but then again, she would have said were-grizzlies were impossible. "You are not going to claim Black Plague."

He shook his head. A quick twist before recentering. "Not that one. Earthquakes and a couple floods. Little enclaves of knowledge just disappear. Lost in holy wars or we don't know why." His nostrils flared then steadied. She got the feeling that while his normal mind was sitting here talking to her, the bear in him kept alert, watching his environment even when he was sitting safely inside a cabin. "Best we understand, magic is incredibly delicate. When too many people mess in it, things go boom."

She stared at him. This was all impossible, especially in this day and age. And yet, wasn't there lots of information on the Internet about magic and the like? *Fairies are real! Get your own pixie dust here!*

He moved awkwardly in his seat. "After centuries of things going wrong, shifters decided to keep it secret or else." He leveled her with a steady look. "You should remember that."

"I'll remember that if only because I hate it when people think I'm an idiot."

He gave her a lopsided smile. "There's that, too."

She took a deep breath. "So no telling Dad."

"Not until Carl says okay. Believe me, we've discussed it. But—"

"He'd want to publish it." There was no doubt in her mind that her father couldn't keep this to himself. And that left her back where she started: confused and without answers. "But what is this all about?"

Mark shrugged. "We think someone is messing with shifter DNA. Two someones, actually. Mad Einstein as Theo calls him—"

"Who?"

"Theo is Becca's adopted son. Kidnapped a few months ago by Mad Einstein so the bastard could do experiments on their shifter DNA."

She recoiled in horror. Becca's son went through that? "That's awful!"

"Yeah." The sound was more growl of fury than word, and she watched Mark struggle for a moment with his anger. His jaw tightened, his shoulders hunched, and there might have been a thickening of the hair on his forearms. But a moment later, he seemed to get himself under control. "The bastard had a partner, too. Crazy Cat Lady."

"You're kidding, right?"

"A traumatized teenager isn't going to give us the best names. All we know is that she was a woman with cat-slit eyes. Best guess from the description is a cougar."

"Cougar-shifter, right? Not an older woman who—"

"Yeah. Shifter."

She raised her hand, cutting him off. He froze and watched her intently while her tequila-sloshed brain reached for whatever it was that teased the edge of her consciousness. "The cat I saw. Right before the attack."

His ears seemed to twitch. Really. But when she looked closer, everything about him appeared human-man normal except for his abnormal stillness.

"What do you remember?" he asked, his question pressed as a low rumble.

She shook her head. "A cougar, I think. Large cat, golden brown fur, gone in a split second."

He waited for her to say more, but she didn't have anything else. Just a quick flash before her world turned completely inside out. "Tell me more about her," she pressed.

He shrugged, the movement obviously forced as he tried to settle his hackles. "Northern Michigan was lousy with cougars until the wolves got pissed off. Skirmish, war, blah blah blah. There's a tentative peace now thanks to Carl, but who knows what's really going on."

Was he serious? He certainly looked so, but the whole thing just boggled her mind. "There was not a war in Michigan."

"There was. A little one. The one major battle was reported as a cult massacre."

She shook her head. "I don't believe it. The cover-up would have to be massive."

He blew out a breath. "Magic likes to be kept secret. No one does it. It just happens."

She chewed on that for a while. "But now I'm in on the secret."

"Yup. But watch what happens when you try to talk to someone about it. There will be a subliminal compulsion to keep mum. Even if you've never lied before in your life, you'll misdirect your own family. You just will."

She opened her mouth to argue, but then thought back. Wasn't that exactly what had happened at the hospital? She'd started to tell her sister about the attack, but hadn't managed to speak about grown men suddenly changing into bears. And when she'd planned on talking to her father, she'd phrased it as a question and allowed him to laugh her into silence. She hadn't planned to keep silent. She just had.

"I don't like not being in control of my actions," she murmured.

"Tell me about it." When her gaze shot to his, he shrugged. "It's something all shifters get used to. Sometimes we just howl at the moon whether we choose to or not."

She frowned. "I thought you don't do that."

"It's an expression, but you're right. Grizzlies don't howl. We kind of moan at it."

She stared at him, trying to decide if he was joking. When his expression turned sheepish, she realized that he was dead serious. He did moan at the moon. She started to laugh, dropping her head back against the couch as she stared at the ceiling. "This is insane."

"I know. But you're safe. I won't let anything happen to you."

She lifted her head. The way he said it was extra heavy. Like he was vowing to defend her unto death or something. "Am I really in that much danger?"

He shook his head. "We've got things covered." He touched his tablet and angled the screen to her. "See? All clear."

Like she could read anything from across the room. She didn't even bother to look closely. She trusted him to keep her safe. That much, at least, was abundantly clear. "Last question," she said. "Tell me the real reason you're dying."

He flinched, and his hands tightened into fists. "Julie—" he began, but she cut him off. The last thing she wanted to do was cause him pain.

"Look, you don't have to talk about it if you don't want to. But I'd really like to know. I can—"

"Next time I turn into a bear, and I'm not coming back."

Her words stopped in her throat, and then she tilted her head, trying to sort through his words. His tone was so matter of fact that he sounded like he was saying he was moving to Los Angeles and going California native. Except he was talking about being a grizzly. "Start again, please. For the nonshifter in the room."

"For some of us—those with too much animal DNA—we lose ourselves in the animal. It's called going feral."

"So can't you just…you know…not?" She asked the question already knowing it couldn't be that simple. "Just don't go animal."

He snorted and pushed out of the chair. "I'll stop the minute you stop breathing. Or having a period. Or I don't know, waking up and brushing your hair every morning. This is a natural cycle. Some of us just have too much beast. I'm one of them. Drew the unlucky DNA straw. I've been holding it off since I was sixteen. And now I've run out of time."

The way he said that number made her pause. Like it was significant. It took her about two seconds to realize what he meant. "You're talking about that night—our night—when we were teens."

He dropped his hands on his hips as he looked out the window. "That's the real reason I ran, Julie. I knew then that I was losing control and I wasn't coming back to human."

She stood up, needing to meet him more eye to eye. "But you did."

"Six weeks later."

She grimaced. Bet that was weird. Living as a bear for a month and a half, and then boom, human again. "What brought you back?"

His lips curved, and he turned to look at her. "A girl with a citrus scent making love to her boyfriend." He shrugged. "You have a citrus scent, Julie. It reminded me of you, and I wanted you. So I changed back. I stood there naked next to their tent, barely able to speak, and hungry as hell."

He was lost in memories, his expression stark as the evening shadows cut into his cheekbones. She stepped closer to him, touching his chest as a way to reach out because he seemed to need it. His breath hitched under her fingers, and his empty hand came up to cover hers. But he didn't look at her.

"Citrus girl called the cops. They came and called my father. By that time, I'd eaten a box of granola bars and had started to think again. You have no idea what it's like to claw your way back into the higher cortex." He closed his eyes. "It's really hard, Julie. And getting harder every time."

And there was her answer. Hadn't she wondered if he was bipolar? The grizzly was the nonverbal guy who answered the door that first time. The one who grunted at her and slammed back coffee like it was the elixir of life. And then there was this man. Quiet, but still articulate. The man who ran a business and installed electronic surveillance equipment around the cabin. And according to him, that man was slipping away.

"There has to be a way to stop it," she said.

"You sound like Carl."

"Maybe you should list—"

He pressed his finger to her lips. It was warm against her skin, and she felt the callus as he brushed gently across her mouth. "Don't make yourself crazy. Carl and I have been looking since the day I came back at sixteen. And there were others long before us. All we've found is vague hints, magical spells." He looked significantly at her. "Fairy tales."

Her father's research.

He nodded, probably reading her understanding off her face. "Did you never wonder why your father started researching shifter tales?"

She snorted. "Who knows what captures my father's attention?"

"I do. *I* did."

She arched her brows, waiting for him to elaborate. Eventually he spoke.

"Your father's family is from here. Generations back."

"Yeah. Great-great-granddad was a traveling salesman or something. Fell in love with a girl here and took her away."

"But they came back now and then. Eventually someone bought this cabin as a summer place."

"The older one burned down. Dad called it a rattrap."

His lips quirked into a brief smile. "Some day I'll tell you exactly what happened to that place." Then before she could ask, he raised his hand. "Wasn't me. Well before my time."

She smiled, pleased to share this short moment of humor even if he wasn't telling her the full truth. "So what did you do?"

"It was the next summer. The one after our night."

"The one I decided to stay with my mother in Chicago and to intern at a law office." It had been the first step in her path to becoming a legal secretary.

"Yeah. I talked to your dad. I really wanted to know about you, about whether or not you were coming back." He sighed as if her decision still depressed him. "When I found out his ancestors were from here, I started asking about his family stories."

Her eyes widened. "You got him started on the local fairy tales!"

"His grandmother had told him about a witch who bound a wolf to her. It gave her the ability to shift into animal form so she could defeat her enemies. And the wolf became a man who fought at her side."

She brought his hand away from her mouth, clasping it between her two. "You think the wolf was a feral and she brought him back."

"Yes. Maybe."

Well, that sounded hopeful. "What happened at the end? Did he stay human? Did she—"

"It's a fairy tale, Julie. Told from the human perspective."

Clearly she was meant to understand what that meant. She hadn't a clue.

"The good guys were the humans. They killed the witch in her wolf form and then burned the man at the stake as a warlock."

"Oh. That sucks."

He flashed her a brief smile. "His interest grew over the years, but it wasn't until this summer that he found more information on that story. Ingredients to a binding spell." He gestured behind him to the kitchen. "We even tried to re-create it."

So that's what that thing in the refrigerator was. She'd found a bottle labeled "Experiment 7" stored behind the beer. It was now on the counter in preparation for the trash. "And? What happened?"

He looked back out the window. From her angle, she could see his head turn slightly as he steadily scanned the environment. "And nothing. I couldn't tell him what I was looking for. I asked for bonding rituals, love spells and the like. I even paid him for the work and drank the potions."

"Seriously?" His silence told her that he had indeed slammed back experiments one through six. "What did you find?"

"A killer case of indigestion and really bad BO." His gaze returned to hers. "And your dad had a heart attack."

Her eyes widened. "He didn't drink them, did he?"

"Only me. And we made sure nothing was poisonous." He gestured to the bottle on the counter. "I'm not supposed to try that one until the next full moon."

Because that made logical sense—not. Meanwhile he turned to look at her dad's office. "There were more recipes that we hadn't tried yet. I've already looked on his desktop. There isn't anything there, so it must have been on his tablet or in his journals."

The missing tablet and journals. This is why he'd been alarmed by the "wrong" scent in the office. This is why he thought someone had stolen the information. Because it might contain the key to him staying human.

"We need to tear this place apart," she said. "We've got to find—"

He shook his head. "I already did that while you were away. They're not here."

Which led credence to the idea that an evil someone had stolen her father's research. "That's why they attacked," she said softly, the pieces falling into place. Not to mention a killer case of the heebie-jeebies. "I'm the only one who can read his notes."

"What?"

"Have you seen my dad's handwriting? It's appalling, and that's when he's not writing in shorthand."

He touched her arm. "Are you saying that whatever was stolen—can't be read?"

"Anything on the tablet is probably understandable. Anything in his journals would look like scribbles." She flashed him a rueful smile. "What did you think I was doing those summers when you excluded me from the fun stuff? I was transcribing my father's notes into English."

"For the record, I wasn't excluding you from fun stuff. I was keeping you away from shifter stuff."

"What?"

"Look, I remember cutting you out. Parties you got uninvited to. Times things broke up just as you arrived."

She stiffened her spine, remembering the pain of that. She'd been a teen in a small town where she didn't go to school. She was a visitor for the summer without even her sister for company because Ellen had wanted science summer school way more than time with their father. That left Julie in Gladwin feeling like she was being snubbed at every turn. She lost track of all the times conversations just stopped when she showed up. And that was nothing compared to the "get together and hang out" times when she wasn't invited or worse, it somehow got canceled only to happen somewhere else. She'd hated it and she'd hated them for being so snobbish. It never occurred to her that it was because of this…this magic business.

But even so, the memory still stung.

"So that was you?"

He snorted. "Hell no. That was Carl or Tonya. Even back then, they were the leaders of our group. But, yeah, I helped enforce it. Julie, you aren't a shifter. No one could have guessed that you would be here now."

It made sense. It did, but logic didn't hold sway over her feelings. "Do you know how outcast I felt?"

"Do you know how outcast we feel? You've got the whole wide world at your feet. Julie, you can go anywhere, be anything."

"So can—"

"We can't," he interrupted. "It's a…a salmon thing even though we're grizzlies. Just like a salmon returns home to spawn, we have to come back to Gladwin throughout our lives. But even if that weren't true, all shifters need a wild place to run. We can't live in big cities. It makes us insane." He touched her chin pulling her around to face him. "Imagine being a teenager and knowing that you can't leave small-town Michigan. That all those big possibilities aren't there for you. You can't be a pilot—what if you shift on a plane? You can't live where big business opportunities exist. You certainly can't go into the military and risk exposing your secret that way. All those little things that you take for granted are triply hard for us because we have to keep our wild nature under control. We have to balance the animal with the human, and that doesn't always work."

"All of life is a balancing act."

"Yeah, we figure that out with maturity. We're talking teenagers here." His fingers caressed her hair. "Yes, we were mean to you. I admit it. But that's because we were so damned jealous of you, we couldn't stand it." He took a breath. "Even me, and believe me, I wanted you from the first moment I saw the book you'd painted on your big toe with polish."

She blinked. She'd forgotten about that. Hell, without friends to hang around with, she'd had plenty of time to decorate her nails.

"You had big eyes and a sharp mind. You wanted to learn everything about the world then, including us—"

"I just wanted some friends."

"And you were going to figure us out. You were going to hear about the magic. And so we excluded you." He took a breath. "I made sure you weren't around us as a group, but I still knew all about you. I still watched where you went and what you did."

She bit her lip, thinking about the times he'd just shown up when she was sitting by a stream reading. Or when she was out for a walk by herself. He'd show up and be nice. More than nice, he'd been sexy and funny, and she'd thought maybe she was finally starting to fit in. But then the next night, she'd hear about another party she hadn't been invited to. Another hangout at the stream that he'd never mentioned.

"You ran so hot and cold. I hated you even as…"

"Even as I wanted you with every breath in my body."

She couldn't believe it. He had yearned for her? He had wanted her? "I felt like you kept toying with me. Being wonderful just to throw me away." Lord, even now she couldn't keep the hurt from her voice.

He leaned in and their foreheads touched. Their breath mingled while his other hand slipped to caress the length of her jaw. "Push/pull," he breathed. "Animal/man. Want/can't have." He cupped her face and lifted her lips to his. But he didn't touch them. He didn't take the kiss she so desperately wanted. "That's my life, Julie. And I'm losing the battle."

"No," she whispered. "No, there has to be an answer."

He shook his head. "I've tried."

She could hear the defeat in his voice. The soul-deep weariness of the struggle. It was the sound of a man giving up. Of one who was going to settle for what little he'd received and try to be content. But Julie wasn't wired that way. Maybe because she hadn't fought this fight her whole life. But she'd just learned that the world was a thousand times bigger than she'd believed a day ago. God only knew what she'd discover tomorrow. And she'd be damned if she let him give up like this. Not when she'd just entered the fight.

"No," she said softly. And when he pulled back, she took hold of his shoulders and drew him forward. "No," she repeated, and then she took his mouth with hers. Forget waiting for him to kiss her. Forget letting this shifter insanity decide how she was going to feel. She'd let the magic exclude her as a teen because she hadn't known better. Well, now she knew. Now she was on board and making changes.

She slammed her mouth against his, and when he gasped in reaction, she thrust her tongue into his mouth. It didn't take him long to react. She'd barely discovered this new bold side of herself when he wrapped his arms around her and drew her flush against him, arching her for his possession.

Thrust, parry, push, pull. Their tongues danced together, and when they finally pulled apart to breathe, her heart was hammering and her legs were liquid.

Well, she thought in a distant part of her mind, apparently she could still be attracted to a man who was part bear. She'd wondered, though it had been a quiet question buried beneath the general WTF of discovering magic. Now she knew that the attraction, at least, was just the same as before. Stronger, even, because now the questions were answered, the inconsistencies made clear.

"Julie," he said, her name a hoarse rasp.

She waited to hear if there was more. Did he have a question for her? Something he wanted to tell her? But the silence stretched on, and when she dared look at him, she saw the desperation in his eyes. The need and…

The defeat. He wanted her but knew that it was only temporary. It was the wish of a dying man. And it thoroughly pissed her off.

"No," she said, her voice firming with sudden conviction. "No, no, no, no, no!"

He backed away, and it took her a moment to realize he thought she was denying him. So she gripped his arm and held him to her. He could break away at any moment, of course. She felt like she had two fingers on a tiny patch of fur on a bear. But she held on with everything she had.

"You are not giving up. You are not slinking off like some whipped dog to die."

He straightened at that. "Do you know how insulting that is?"

"I don't care," she said. "Look, you want to find some magic potion to keep you human? Well, this is the age of the Internet." She cracked her knuckles. "We're going to find it."

He sighed. "Julie, we've been looking—"

"Don't care, Mark. *I* haven't been looking. You need someone with experience in anthropology and folktales and I don't know what. That's my father."

"We can't bring him in."

"Without him, you'll just have to settle for me. I'm his daughter, can read his nutso shorthand, and I'm motivated." She stepped forward, getting right up into his face. Close enough to touch him. Close enough to grip his hard dick, if she wanted to. And she really wanted to. But she held her hands firmly on her hips. This wasn't about sex, this was about fighting for his life. And once he had a life—and a future—then they could see about the hot sex part. And the-happily-ever-after part. But that couldn't even be on the table until they solved this.

"Are you with me, Mark? Are you willing to keep searching?"

He took a deep breath, his expression haunted. And for the first time, she saw the depths to which he'd sunk in despair. What would it be like to search since you were sixteen for the miracle solution to your life? To fight for answers, to hold on to hope, only to be disappointed time and time again? And here she was, at the eleventh hour, asking him to believe again. Asking him to give up the peace that came with acceptance and try again.

"Please, Mark. Can you please hold on to hope one last time?"

"There's no reason to think you can succeed where everyone else has failed," he said softly. "And lots of reasons to say you haven't a prayer."

She swallowed. That was true. After all, according to him, shifters had been searching for the solution to the feral problem for centuries. What could she add that no one else could?

"I—" she began, trying to find a reason he could believe in. Something other than, *Because I want to believe I can.*

"Okay," he said.

She blinked. "What?"

He drew her hands up to his mouth, pressing kisses into her knuckles. "Julie, this morning was a miracle. I wanted to see you again to explain. And to have you not only listen but to…" His cheeks tinged red.

"To hump like bunnies?"

He grinned. "Yeah. Miracle."

She felt her cheeks heat. "It was pretty awesome for me, too."

"So you already came loaded with one miracle. What's to say you can't pull off another?"

Logic? Reason? But they were talking about magic, so she decided to toss those two scientific strategies out the window. "Exactly," she said, pretending to a confidence she really didn't feel. "We can figure this out. I'm sure of it."

He took a deep breath. "Where do we start?"

Good question. It was too late to call her father and ask about whatever research he'd had on his tablet. That meant going back over what ground her father already had established before they started looking deeper. "Fire up that dinosaur of a desktop. I still have that creepy thumb drive of his notes." She froze a moment, only now understanding the significance of a bear with a little bullet hole in its chest. "Oh my God—"

He held up his hand, stopping her explosion. "Graveyard humor. I thought it was funny."

Well, she didn't. But rather than argue, she pulled out her phone. "Actually, Dad often stays up late reading. Maybe he's awake."

She texted him, not wanting to disturb his sleep. But if he was awake, then maybe she could get a jump on things now. "U up, Dad? I'm with Mark. Got questions."

Five seconds her phone rang.

"Dad?"

"What's up, honey? I'm so bored I'm willing to eat hospital food. What do you want to know?"

With a grin, she gave Mark a thumbs-up. "Hold on while I grab something to write on. Mark has been talking to me about your research, and I've got some questions…"

Chapter 13

Three days later, Mark had to go furry or kill something. He was sitting slumped on Julie's couch. His eyes were bleary, and his shoulders ached. Usually, he reached for food or caffeine at this point, but he hadn't the strength. Plus, his stomach rebelled at the idea of more carrots and dip, to say nothing about that disaster called store-bought hummus and crackers.

He used to think exhaustion was the best cure for his twitchy growly side. No such luck. It just brought his bear closer to the surface. He could step outside and smell the clean Michigan air, but he feared he'd sprout a snout as he did it. So he waited, trying to ride out the violent impulses.

Then he glanced across the room to Julie, who was sitting at the kitchen table. She was taking notes as she scrolled through God only knew what on her tablet while slamming back crap coffee like it was a protein shake. Which it definitely wasn't.

Focus on her face. On the human details.

Sloppy ponytail and peanut butter smudge at the edge of her mouth. Stale coffee on her lips and grizzly hunch that wasn't really grizzly. Her shoulders would ache, and he prowled forward to rub them. To rub her. Without even seeing her eyes, he knew they were tinged with red and that she was developing a permanent line between her brows.

Human details. Human life. How far away it felt and yet every moment, so precious.

Mate. Now.

They had been. Every night in a frenzy of coupling that was the only reason his bear tolerated three days of research.

Outside. Run free.

Simple choice. Mate or run wild. She was the only thing keeping him from going feral. She was his only touchstone to keeping him sane.

The phone rang, startling her and making him growl deeply. She glanced at him as she grabbed the phone, then kept her worried eyes on him as she chatted casually with her family. Her father was doing fine, but his continued fever kept him in the hospital.

Reassure her. Smile.

He did, though he had to remember how. She nodded, accepting the lie. And while he focused on the tension in his body, he realized she'd out-endured him and that was freaking impressive. He also saw what his friends did when they looked at him.

He, too, had gone through bouts of intense concentration. The drive to the find an answer had consumed him. He didn't eat, didn't sleep, and never spoke without a growl. He'd coded his first program in that state. He thought if he could create a computerized hunting simulation, it would ease that ants-under-his-skin need to get out and go animal.

It had worked…for a time.

He'd slept and eaten. He'd believed in a happily-ever-after. Until it had stopped working. It was all a lie. He'd never find relief. God hated him.

Eventually he tried again. Next came DNA studies. Carl's research into magic. Maybe the answer was in fairy tales. Magic potions? Elation—depression—intense work—elation. A never-ending cycle. Highs were fragile. Lows got deeper, blacker. And always the temptation to surrender to the beast.

Take her. Now.

His dick was thick and hot. In a minute, he'd give in to the need. He'd stumble to the bathroom and flip on the shower. And while the hot water pounded his body, he'd imagine mounting Julie. She'd be a large, healthy brown bear, and he'd take her over and over until he growled and released. He didn't do this with her. The need to be fur and claws as he spurted was too much, and he was ashamed. So he hid in the bathroom and found relief.

For a time. Until the need tore at him again. How long did he have this time? A few hours? A day? How long could he hold off until he lost control, became a bear, and took from Julie what she wasn't willing to give?

He focused on her face again. *Human.*

He saw panic in her eyes. A desperation that told him she was on his same merry-go-round of hope, desperation, and despair. It was consuming her, and it would kill him to watch it.

He rolled his neck and flexed his fingers, feeling the grizzly reassert itself with every rumbling breath. He watched her eyes widen and she ended her conversation. He hadn't the human ability to hear what she said. He managed one word.

"Julie." And then he was on her.

She was used to it by now, but he still despised himself for it. No words, no tenderness, just need—raw and animal.

She put the condom on him.

He bent her facedown over the table.

If he went furry, then thank God she couldn't see it.

Mate.

He poured himself into her.

And when he came back to himself, when words formed and his hands were hands not paws, he found himself kissing her back, licking her shoulder blades while he stroked her clit. No danger of too long a claw now. And he rode out her orgasm while still embedded within her.

Mate.

And he exploded again.

* * *

"As long as we're taking a break, I have questions."

Mark grunted, his focus already dwindling now that he couldn't directly see Julie. She was in the kitchen and he could hear her readjusting her clothing. He was in the bathroom, making sure that all parts of his mind and body were human again.

"Do shifters react especially strongly to any type of food or metal or something? Silver? Gold?"

"Frankincense and myrrh?" he asked as he stepped out from the bathroom.

Damn, she was fully dressed again, a light sundress that even a grizzly could shove out of the way. Any hint of their antics were in the flush to her cheeks and the open space on the table. "Yeah. Do they—"

"No. And lead bullets kill as easily as silver. But we do have stronger systems, heal a little faster, are a bit harder to take down."

"That doesn't help."

"It does if you're being chased by a hunter with a shotgun."

She stiffened, and he regretted his words immediately. "I'm teasing. That's never happened to me."

"Liar," she said, though the word was muffled as he pulled her against his chest. He hadn't even consciously crossed the room, but now he was nuzzling into her hair and filling his mind with her scent.

"No, really," he said as he licked the curve of her ear. "It was a pistol, not a shotgun. And he was a terrible shot."

"Not helping."

"Tell me what you need, baby," he said, though the words sounded more like a rumble of vibration than words. "Anything. It's yours."

She straightened slowly, pushing away from him with a steady hand. He had to consciously relax his muscles to give her six inches of space. "You have to stop, Mark. I'll never get any more work done and there's a ton—"

"Good. Because we're done for the night."

Every inch of her body stiffened. "This is your life, Mark—"

"I know what's at stake. Better than you."

She nodded, her eyes too wide in the early evening shadows. "Yeah," she grudgingly admitted, "I guess you do."

"I've been facing this for a very long time."

"I'm not giving up."

He could see that. It was written boldly in every line of her body. "Didn't ask that. But we're taking a break."

She grimaced, but eventually nodded. "Okay. Is there a pizza delivery place nearby? Let's order—"

"No."

She arched a brow. "Hate pizza?"

He chuckled. "I spent at least a month eating only that."

"So now you're sick of it?"

He almost laughed, but the sound stuck in his throat. "No," he said softly. "I'm sick of just surviving. Pushing hard on adrenaline and determination. That's no way to live, Julie."

"But—"

He caressed her jaw, holding her gaze with a ferocity that he feared would frighten her. "I don't want to die. I don't want to go bear and never come back."

"So let's keep working—"

"But I won't spend my last days working and eating crap. If I've only got a few more sunrises—"

"Don't say that!"

"Then let me spend this sunset having a wonderful dinner with a beautiful woman."

She blinked quickly, but not before he saw the sheen of tears in her eyes. Then she released a low snort. "I'll need a shower and some serious makeup before I even approach beautiful."

He studied her face, memorizing every glorious feature including the acne scars and the furrow between her brows. He saw the mole near her hairline and the extra fullness to her mouth. And every imperfection added up to the most beautiful face he'd ever seen in his life because of all of it was her. Fierce, determined Julie.

"You're beautiful," he said, meaning it to the depths of his soul.

"You're hallucinating from malnutrition."

He laughed. "Carrots and hummus do not sustain a guy like me."

"Don't forget the Ho Hos."

Oh, yes. Those were great, but those ran out hours ago. "A mere bite."

"Exactly—"

"Julie, I need you to hear this, okay? You are so beautiful, I can't even express it. I like how you look. I like the way your hair curls around your ears. I like the full hourglass figure. I love the large breasts and hips. And I—" He cut himself off before he said the rest. Before he admitted to himself and her that he was falling in love. Because that spelled disaster to a doomed man. And it meant even worse things for the woman he'd leave behind. So he swallowed that part and substituted something vastly less real. "And I need to take you out to an expensive dinner and dessert. Right now."

Her eyes shone bright, but she didn't look away. "No shower?"

"Can I join you in there?"

She snorted. "We'd never make it out of the house."

"Oh, well in that case…" He let his voice trail off suggestively.

She wasn't having any of it. She pushed away from him and he counted it a huge victory that he let her go. "Ten minutes," she said. "Well, maybe twenty."

"Fifteen. And I'll shower in your father's bathroom."

She was already halfway up the stairs. "Good idea."

He frowned. It was hard to focus when her ass moved like that. "Are you saying I stink?"

"Does a grizzly shit in the woods?"

His mind scrambled to replay her words. She was laughing as she rounded the top and heading toward the bathroom. And he…he was stunned. She'd just made a shifter joke. A lame one, but still…What normal had ever accepted the shifter world so quickly and so easily? Especially after her traumatic introduction.

God, she was one impressive woman. Now all he had to do was figure out how exactly he could stay human long enough to get his fill of her. Probably only take a few hundred years…

* * *

Julie took twenty-seven minutes to get ready. Shower and sundress were easy, but the accessories took some time. Especially since she hadn't packed for a date night. She could only thank heaven that she'd thrown some makeup into her bag out of habit, not intention. And while she curled her hair away from her eyes, she contemplated her lack of jewelry.

She hadn't brought any from home, but there were pieces left over from when she was a teenager. Wild flights of fancy and daring costume jewelry that suited someone a lot bolder than the woman she'd grown into. But what the hell? Mark made her feel bold. And so she put on the huge gold hoop earrings and decided to go for broke with the necklace.

The pendant was a simple glass drop in lightest blue shot with gold. It dangled from a cheap chain, but it plunged all the way down her ample cleavage. She'd had plenty as a teen, but now as a woman? She had big mounds that (thankfully) Mark seemed to like. And the teardrop drew the eye to her massive assets.

She was nervous as she came down the stairs, but the look in his eyes was like the prom night she'd never had. His eyes widened. She saw his mouth drop a little open, and his hand squeezed the railing. He looked like he was going to climb up the stairs and carry her to bed where he would ravish her all night long. And at that moment, she wondered what exactly she wanted. Because ravishment sounded pretty damn good to her. Especially since she could see the indecision on his face. He wanted her and it was taking every bit of his control not to take her.

She'd never felt that from anyone before. Such intensity. Such absolute hunger but held in check by an iron control. Made everything inside her go liquid with want. And then he held out his hand to her, so she descended the last few steps feeling like a queen entering her court.

"I'm am the luckiest man alive," he said as he nuzzled beneath her ear. "You smell amazing."

"I am never changing this shampoo ever."

He licked her. A light quick flick of his tongue before he rumbled his answer. "It's not the shampoo. It's you."

What had she done right in her life to deserve this man? This *magical* man. Sure, he turned into a grizzly, and, frankly, she wondered where was her sanity. Who wanted to get involved with a bear? One who had a death sentence coming in a very, very short time.

Her. She wanted to. She wanted him. And rational or not, she was along for the ride for as far as it could take her.

"So," she asked as they headed for the door. "Where are we going?"

"It's a restaurant a ways from here. That's the problem with Gladwin. Nothing fancy for miles."

She hesitated. "Are you sure you want to take the time? Dad might be coming home tomorrow and that'll make it harder—"

"I'm sure. Stop worrying. Start living." He flashed her his teeth. "With me."

She stiffened in mock insult. "Why, Mr. Robertson, are you asking an innocent girl like me to move in with you? What would my father say?"

His eyes crinkled as he smiled. "Probably, can she help with my research?"

She snorted. "That's probably true. I don't think Dad cared about the niceties of polite society even when he was in polite society."

He opened his truck door for her and helped her climb in. It was sweet and courtly, and she couldn't have been more pleased if she were stepping into a limousine. Then he popped around the other side, and soon they were on the road.

"Was your father really in polite society?" he finally asked.

"Absolutely. Remember that traveling salesman? He made it big with the Crescent Brass and Pin Company. Not Henry Ford kind of money, but he did just fine. According to family legend, his daughter became a society matron."

"But your dad was probably an academic when he was still in diapers."

"Much to the despair of the women who kept trying to make him into a dashing young lad."

"So how did your parents meet?"

"School, of course. University of Michigan. Dad liked her practical side. She kept him on track, grounded him when he was prone to lose himself in his research."

"And what did she see?"

"A romantic. Flowers, poetry, and badly sung ballads in the moonlight." Julie sighed. "They divorced when I was a teen. Turns out poetry pales when someone's forgotten to pay the water bill."

"Ouch." He looked at her, his eyes narrowing. "Which side do you favor? Practical or romantic?"

"You can't guess?" She didn't mean to test him, but it was an old habit with her. Had he really been paying attention? Or had everything they'd done been an elaborate dance for ulterior reasons?

"Oh, you're practical through and through," he said glibly. "Pay your bills on time, have a boring car and a responsible job."

Then he flashed her a heated look that set her blood on simmer. "But you give your heart easily and too well. Romantics like that get taken for a ride. So you try to be logical, but then it happens again. A guy shows up with flowers and pretty words, and there you go."

She swallowed, her throat suddenly dry. Damn, he'd nailed it right on the head. Except this time it wasn't pretty words and flowers that had caught her heart. This time, she'd tumbled head-long into a man of magic. "Makes me sound like a sap," she said as she turned to look out the trees whipping past the window.

"It's a miracle, Julie. Do you know how hard it is for me to connect?" His voice was calm. As steady and even as the freeway they'd pulled onto. "Animals love instinctively with very few. Child or mate, that's it. Everything else is food or rival. Carl's my best friend, but the minute we became teens, my bear started to assert itself. Carl's the alpha of my generation, but to my bear, he's the man who's going to kill me when the time comes. At best, he's a rival. At worse, he's my predator."

"That's awful."

"That's animal. Don't get me wrong. Animals feel love, especially pets. But I'm a wild animal. It's the man who makes human connections, and even before my teens it was hard."

She twisted in her seat, needing to see his face as the talked. "Why?"

"Because my parents were shifters. Strong ones who shouldn't have mated. But the drive hit and nine months later, I was born. They tried to make it work for my sake. Mom stuck around long enough to get me out of diapers, but in the end the wanderlust got her. Or at least that's what Dad says. I don't remember her."

"None of this is in your bio," she said. He shot her a surprised look, and she shrugged. So yeah, maybe she'd read every inch of his company website. It was mostly gaming stuff, but his bio was front and center in her mind. Plus Ellen might have sent her links to every article about him. Which was a lot. "It talks about a glorious childhood in a welcoming community."

"That's all true. The Gladwin grizzly clan raised me. Plus, Dad stuck around, and his girlfriends helped. Carl's mom was a steady female until she died. All in all, a good childhood."

"And yet you say you can't connect easily. If at all."

He nodded. "I can't. I try. I talk to people. I look them in the eyes and fight for the empathy."

"And what happens?"

He shook his head. "I don't know. It's just not there." Then he looked at her. "Except with you. Except every moment I look at you, I want you."

She sighed, knowing the truth now. Hearing it loud and clear. "That's mating, isn't it? The instinct to carry on the species."

"Yes."

Talk about stabbing her in the heart. It hurt so bad that she had to turn away.

"But I think it's more. We connected when we were teens. Do you remember eating ice cream together? I do. I remember what you wore, how you laughed, and how I wanted to lick the chocolate sauce off your lips."

"Horny teen."

He didn't even deny it. "But I knew I wasn't getting laid. I knew you lived in Chicago and whatever happened would be temporary. We had nothing in common and I couldn't tell you anything about who and what I really was. I didn't care. I just wanted to be with you. I still do."

None of this made sense. On the one hand he sounded like he was warning her off. Reminding her every way possible that a relationship between them was doomed. He didn't connect. His only attraction to her was the instinctive need to mate. And then he said despite all those things, there was something else. Something that drew him to her, that made him want to be with her outside of animal hunger.

"Why?" she pressed. God, she just wanted to know where she stood with him. "What makes me so special?"

"You just are. In every way, you just are."

That wasn't a satisfying answer, though only a fool expected a man to be articulate about his feelings. Still, his words resonated with her. He sounded sincere, and though she'd been fooled before, he'd done everything he could to dissuade her from an attachment. Was it his fault—or hers—if she felt special when she was around him? He made her believe in her own beauty when he was beside her.

"Okay," she said softly. Then she repeated it with more strength. "Okay. I'm awesome. You're magical. Let's go eat something really fattening."

He looked over at her, his lips curving into a slow, sexy smile. "Yes," he said. "Exactly that. Yes."

So they did. They had steak and cheesecake. They chowed on hot rolls with butter and tiny salads because it was served with the meal. And they talked. He wanted to know everything about her job and her plans for the future. She delved deep into his thoughts about his company and where he would take it if he had all the time and money in the world. They talked about her college and his lack. And by the time she was waddling back to the truck from being overstuffed on good food, they were laughing together like old, dear friends.

Well, old, dear friends who wanted desperately to get into each other's pants.

And when she struggled in her now-tight dress to climb into his truck, he swept her into his arms and lifted her inside. She squealed, of course, and laughed as she threw her arms around him. He was strong and she had tumbled headlong into love. She didn't want to admit that to herself. Didn't want to acknowledge the way the moonlight made his hair glow like magic or that she could drown in the mystical blue of his eyes. So rather than think, she kissed him. She pulled him close when he set her down in the cab, and she let herself play with his mouth, the contours of his chest, and the hard ridge of his cock through his jeans.

It didn't take him long to respond. Not when he began to growl his words and lick her face. She thought she'd be repulsed by the way his bear took over when they made love. But the way he touched her was all need. Fingers, tongue, teeth—all of it everywhere.

Thrilling.

She couldn't stop stroking him, and he returned the favor to her breasts. Oh wow, she loved it when he touched her like that. She arched into him, loving the squeeze of his large hands.

Needing the pinch on her nipples. And wishing they were home already. Wishing…

He separated her knees simply by pressing closer. Then it was a simple matter to brush aside her skirt and stroke her wet panties. She jolted at the feel and grabbed his shoulders to steady herself.

"Get me home," she said against his mouth.

He'd dropped his mouth to her neck, scraping his teeth across her flesh as both his hands found their way to between her thighs. "Citrus honey," he murmured. Then he ripped the thin cotton apart.

She jolted as he suddenly stroked her without the fabric barrier. "Did you just—"

"Come for me," he said as he pushed a thick finger inside her.

"Here?" she squeaked even as her body tightened around his invasion. Not to restrict him, but to pull him in deeper.

"It's late," he said. "No one is around. And even if they were, I'm blocking the view."

"But—" she squeaked again. She couldn't think with him between her thighs. Not when he pinched her clit. "But…" she tried again, her mind stuttering over the objections. They were outside. They were in public. She might have gotten over the fear of him seeing her naked, but random strangers?

He eased back on his sensual assault, though he still kept it going with slow thrusts with his fingers and even slower strokes over her clit. Then he lifted his mouth to whisper in her ear. "You're with a wild animal now, Julie. And he wants to lick your come off his fingers. He wants to hear you cry out. And he doesn't want to wait."

Oh, wow. Just... wow.

"Does it excite you to know how much I want that? That I don't care who knows or who sees? I just want you orgasming all around me. Right now."

It did. Oh, wow, did she ever want that.

"Tell me, Julie. Tell me you want—"

"Only if I get to return the favor right afterwards. Only if you climb into the driver's seat and let me suck you dry." She'd never wanted to do that in all her life. She'd never thought she'd be a woman to sit in a dark parking lot with her head bobbing up and down on a man's lap. And yet, she did. The public setting. The hot need. All if it combined to make her want to do everything and more. Right now.

He didn't wait to answer. She felt it in the sudden thrust of his fingers deep inside her. She took everything he gave her. Especially when he played her clit like a drum. She didn't even know how he did it, but he set up a beat and he kept tapping out a tempo that drove her wild. Slow, fast, feather light, then heavy push. Her legs were spread as wide as she could make them and he was wedged between them as far in as he could fit. And still the drumbeat rolled through her body like thunder. Wild. Unpredictable.

Explosion.

She came with a startling choke in a moment between breaths. She came while he was trying to slow it down. She came while he had three fingers inside her, and she kept coming in waves of energetic pulses that exploded outward from where he was embedded deep.

And when she flopped backward in the cab, completely boneless and satiated, he slowly withdrew his fingers and licked them clean. He would have licked her, too, if she'd let him. He would have spread her right there and tasted her to another explosive orgasm, but she held him off.

Instead, she touched his chin, forcing him to look at her while she bit her lip then gave him a coy smile. Lord, who was this hungry tart? A woman who did scandalous things in a parking lot? She was finally throwing off embarrassment and self-doubt. Look at her, indulging in things completely of the body and reveling in every scandalous second.

So she lifted one leg and set it on his chest, steadily pushing him away.

"Get in the cab," she ordered. "It's my turn now."

His eyes widened and his nostrils flared. "You know you're making every single one of my adolescent fantasies come true."

"Good. Because once I'm done with yours, we're going to start on mine."

Chapter 14

He didn't take her back to her father's cabin. He took her to his home. He carried her into his basement den and set her on the massive bed. And when she told him she was able to walk all on her own, he made it his mission to make sure she couldn't.

They did, indeed, work on fantasies, and she was as saucy as she'd never been. And as shy as she feared she might. It didn't matter. He met her wherever she was, coaxed her or demanded of her until she spent an incredible amount of time screaming around his pounding cock. And if it wasn't the moment for screaming Os, they cuddled together and murmured confessions while sharing slow kisses.

She didn't know it was possible to spend a night like this. She hadn't thought a man would ever want to linger over every second whether in a blissful doze or casual laughter. The whole night was magical, and the day never penetrated his bedroom cave.

He fed her when they got hungry. They showered when things got sticky. And if it weren't for the persistent buzz of her phone, she would have remained in this idyll forever. But her phone did buzz and her father was in the hospital, so she had to answer even if it was the last thing she wanted to do.

"Hello?" she rasped.

Mark murmured his protest against the small of her back. He was spooned against her, but had fallen lower along her spine when she reached for her phone.

"Did I wake you?" her sister's voice was disruptive to her bliss. But that was a sacrifice she had to make for family. Sometimes.

"This better be important," she growled to her sister. "Otherwise I'm hanging up."

"Dad's getting discharged. I've got to go back to the lab, but Mom's going to drive him to the cabin. Should arrive around four."

Julie came fully awake with painful intensity. "Today?"

"At four."

She looked at the clock. It was almost noon. "Okay," she said, pretending that panic wasn't clawing at her throat. "No problem."

"So get your hot, slutty self out of bed, kiss that man hard, then go clean up the evidence before Dad gets there. Don't want him having another heart attack, right?"

Julie straightened up, accidentally dislodging Mark. "I was not…" Except she had been. "I *am* not…" Well, she was and she'd liked it. "Oh, shut up!"

She hung up on her sister's peal of laughter. So Dad was coming home. He was better enough to be nursed night and day by her. This was good news, right? She'd wanted her father strong and healthy.

"Your father's been discharged," Mark said as he rubbed sleep out of his eyes. He looked rumpled and sexy and…Hmmmm. He was very hard. And she was very wet.

"You've turned me into a sex addict."

His eyes darkened, and his lips curved. She didn't see him move, but she felt his hand caress her. It had been on her thigh, but now curved between her legs. The movement was slow but absolutely undeniable.

"How long do we have?" he asked.

"Until four. But I need to clean up the place. Get groceries and stuff."

"Hmmm. That'll take about an hour."

"Plus a shower and…and…" He pushed her onto her back, spreading her knees as he kissed a trail down her stomach. "And I think there's plenty of time."

She felt him smile against her belly. "That's what I think, too."

And that was the last thinking she did for a good long, fabulous time.

But even great sex has to end sometime. They showered at his place, then headed to the grocery store. She said nothing about all the elaborate tricks he had in his house to make sure the man was in charge and not the grizzly. Why further ruin the moment? Especially when she didn't need a big yellow sign to tell her that their time was running out. So they shopped in quiet accord and headed back to her father's home. Mark was carrying the bags and she was unlocking the cabin door when it happened. Simple and quick.

She heard some pops. Almost simultaneous, but not quite. A sharp pain hit her back. Mark might have grunted. Maybe. It was hard to tell what with her legs going out and the porch coming up to slap her in the face.

Chapter 15

Mark woke with a stench in his nose and a roar of fury burrowing out of his throat. He didn't even know why he was pissed yet, but he was angry and filled with adrenaline. Except that the sound he created was more of a moan and when he leapt to his feet to scan the environment, all he really did was contract his belly and lift what felt like ten tons on his chest.

Holy shit.

He dragged his eyes open by a supreme act of will and when he couldn't focus, the terror inside him grew exponentially.

"Calm down, Mark. You're safe. The environment is safe." Carl's voice, and it soothed his immediate panic.

"Now wake the shit up. We need your help." That was Tonya, her voice tight with anxiety.

He drew his focus together, forced himself to think. Oddly, his bear was dead asleep, making him the most human he'd ever felt. Which ought to reassure him, but instead made him feel disconnected from himself. The grizzly was so dominant in his mind all the time that this absence unsettled him.

"Give him a minute," another voice said. A stranger. Female. He blinked, focusing on a pert nose covered in freckles. A young redhead with a surprisingly warm smile. She was dressed in a paramedic's uniform.

"Julie?" he asked, his voice coming out as a croak.

The paramedic leaned forward. "Let's start with the basics. What's your name—"

"What the fuck happened?" interrupted Tonya.

Then he saw Carl lean into his field of vision, a bottle of water extended. That's what he needed. He reached for it, his arms leaden. He tried to sit up but failed. What the hell was wrong with him?

"Take it slow," the woman said, though she thankfully helped him sit up. "Does anything hurt?"

"No," he said, more scared than he wanted to admit. "I'm so weak."

Carl squatted down beside him, handing over the water and steadying Mark's hand. "You got hit by tranq darts. A lot of them."

"Julie?" he repeated as he looked around. There were spilled groceries on the ground, bags he'd dropped when he fell. Focusing toward the cabin, he saw Julie's father sitting on the step looking haggard. Beside him stood a middle-aged woman clenching her fists. Her eyes had the crazy intensity of someone barely holding it together, and he knew he was looking at Julie's mother. "Where the hell is Julie?" he said, his voice growing stronger.

"We don't know," Carl said, his voice low but with that steady patience that made him a great alpha. "What do you remember?"

"Groceries," he said. "We went grocery shopping and she bought…" *Oh, crap.* "Garlic and oregano."

"Why does that matter?" Julie's mother asked, her voice tight with worry.

It didn't matter except that it explained why he hadn't smelled the bastards first thing. He'd been carrying the groceries and the spices had masked any other smell. "Stupid," he muttered. He'd been so damned stupid. He'd been relaxed and happy as hadn't happened ever. "So damned—"

"Yeah, stupid. Whatever," Tonya said as she squatted down beside him. "Because everyone expects to be attacked by guys with dart guns. Get your head out of your guilt and start *helping.*"

Tactless, thy name is Tonya. But it worked. He pulled his focus together and looked to the car. Unfortunately, the quick shift made his brain and vision slosh about, and he had to grip Carl's arm as a wave of dizziness rolled through him. But even fighting the nausea, he was able to grit out, "Tablet. Car."

Tonya held it out. "Already got it, but it's password protected."

Right. And why the hell hadn't he noticed it was in her hand the whole time? He needed to get it together. "Give it here," he said, trying to hold out his hand. Tonya didn't even blink.

"Password?"

"Fine." He rattled it off, wondering if any of them would realize his password was Julie plus the date they'd gotten together when they were sixteen. Tonya's eyebrows rose, but she keyed it in. Carl just squeezed Mark's hand.

"We'll find her," he said softly.

And there it was, the information he'd already known. He'd been knocked out. Julie had been taken. If she'd been killed, Tonya wouldn't be so keyed up about him helping because there was nothing he could do. But with Julie missing, he had to get up. He had to find her.

"Slow down, big guy," the paramedic said. "You conked your head pretty good and we don't know what was in those darts."

"So analyze the darts," he growled as he struggled to his feet. Thankfully Carl knew better than to stop him and he kept the petite redhead back.

"We need to get you to a hospital."

"Not happen—"

"Mark!" Carl interrupted. "There's nothing you can do here. Get yourself—"

"Got ya!" Tonya crowed, silencing everyone.

Everyone shifted, trying to look over her shoulder at the tablet. Even Julie's parents came off the porch. Fortunately, Mark was the largest and the closest. He reached around and angled the tablet so he could see the replay of the recordings.

And there was Julie laughing as she fumbled with the front-door lock. Rusty piece of shit. He should have upgraded that when he put in all the surveillance equipment. But in his stupid mind, he'd thought that anything that delayed bad guys from entering the house was a good thing. He hadn't thought that she'd be slowed down.

There wasn't any audio on the feed so he couldn't hear the pops. His memory supplied them, though, the sound of multiple guns going off almost simultaneously. Then a heavy dart appeared in her back and Julie crumpled like a rag doll.

He released a sound, half growl, half whine. It was low and feral, but it came from the man in him, not the grizzly who was still bizarrely quiet. In his peripheral vision, he saw Carl glance nervously in his direction, but he didn't say anything. His gaze was still glued to the tablet screen as two guys in hoodies and baseball caps trotted up the front steps. One continued inside the house. The other leaned over Julie, roughly checking her for weapons. She was unconscious, but it still pissed him off to see how the bastard manhandled her, lingering too long, feeling up her breasts.

"Keep it together," Carl murmured in his ear.

Mark didn't move his gaze. "Leave it alone. My grizzly is asleep."

Tonya and Carl both reacted to that, their heads snapping up at almost the same instant. Mark only cared because it destabilized the viewing screen. So he grabbed the tablet, watching intently as the one bastard flipped Julie over his shoulder. Thoughts spun through his brain without restraint. The guy was shifter strong, barely winded as he lifted her. He had a torn Levi's on, and why the hell did that matter? Julie looked gorgeous, even upside down and unconscious. Bastard patted her behind as he headed down the porch step. Think of something! No fucking clue anywhere. The other one emerged from the house. Also with the same kind of Levi's on. Front porch needed a good sanding and water-resistant stain treatment. Jerk number two was carrying all their research including Carl's older-than-shit spell book.

Perched precariously on top of the book was the magic potion, experiment seven. It was a near duplicate of number six but with the proportions shifted.

"Damn," murmured Carl while Tonya twisted the tablet so she could see better.

"What is that?" she asked. "Why would they take it?"

Did Tonya always ask questions in pairs? And WTF was wrong with him? His mind was spinning out of control. He couldn't focus!

"Mark!" Tonya snapped. "What is that?"

A tablet. A stupid question. A book. What the hell was she asking? Focus! "Bonding rituals. A love potion." Mark took control of the tablet again to scroll through the video from the other cameras with a shaking hand. His mind was spitting out random facts—clouds in the sky, loose roofing tile—without any kind of sense. It ratcheted up the panic inside him because he couldn't think his way through.

"Mark, are you sure? It's completely quiet? Mark!"

Someone was speaking. Carl. Alpha. Smelled like sex and Becca. Don't think about that! Where the hell was Julie?

"Where's your bear, Mark?"

"Gone," he grunted. Fast-forwarded through the feed from front camera one. Pretended he wasn't freaking out. Too many words in his brain and no feelings. Front camera showed a great view of spilled groceries and his ass laid out like a drunk. Lazy shit. Three darts sticking out of his body. Enough tranquilizers to drop a grizzly. As a human he'd been asleep before he hit the ground.

He watched a third asshole crouch over him, a pistol hanging loose while he talked into a cell. Cheap-ass stupid phone. Burner. Probably getting instructions from someone. The trees had that rich green of summer. Can't hear the birds on the video. Eventually, the man straightened up, kicked him in side for good measure, and then joined the guy hauling all the research. Fuckers.

Mark breathed hard, feeling the pull in his swollen side. Bastard should have killed him because nothing was going to stop Mark from killing them now. Not when the three started walking off together, clearly making crude comments about Julie.

"How quiet?"

Nothing was fucking quiet. His brain was a whirlwind of thoughts. He queued up camera- two footage and started fast-forwarding. There had to be something, somewhere. He saw Julie's parents drive up and get out of their car. Nice blue SUV. Rental. Her mom ran to him while the professor hauled out his cell phone and probably dialed 911.

"Mark!"

"What?"

"Your grizzly."

"Asleep. As in nothing." No roar. No fury. No hunger. *Oh shit, shit, shit, shit*—a silent thrum of panic. And simultaneously, why the panic? This was great, wasn't it? Shit, shit, shit.

Carl grabbed his wrist. "Could you shift?"

Mark tried to grab at his bear, but ended up clutching random ridiculous thoughts. Honey. Coffee. Breeze. Tablet. Julie. Julie!

"No," he snapped. And damn it, he felt completely out of control like this. Like without his bear to focus him, he was spinning wildly, which left him vulnerable and Julie lost. How he'd prayed for a few moments respite from his grizzly, but now that it was silent, he was insane with panic.

Tonya and Carl exchanged glances, but didn't say anything. Meanwhile, Mark queued up the next camera feed and started running through it, pretending to a focus he didn't have.

Meanwhile, Carl started barking orders. "I want an analysis of those darts immediately."

"Yeah, I guessed," Tonya said as the paramedic handed the things over. "You'll want blood work and stuff, too," she said as they looked at Mark.

Camera showed squirrels. Leaves. Rocks. No Julie. No help. Get it together.

"Mark, we need you to go to the hospital."

"No."

Someone touched his arm, and he flinched. He had to watch the video feed. He had to find Julie.

"Mark, think. Your bear is *quiet*."

He was thinking too damned much! "I know—" He was so absorbed in watching footage that he didn't process the words for a moment. But then the significance hit him. Some drug had quieted the grizzly to the point of absolute silence. And, yeah, it knocked the man out, but the grizzly was staying down while he was up and thinking. Granted, it was out-of-control thoughts, but still. This is was important if he could just focus.

Never since he was a teenager had the man been alone in his brain. And if this were possible—if there was a medication or something—that could do this without knocking him unconscious for hours on end? Well, that was good, right? Not only could it be a temporary staying measure for himself and all ferals, but the break it would give to teenage shifters was enormous. With all those hormones zipping around in an adolescent's body, even a temporary pause from the demands of the animal inside would be a godsend.

But...Julie!

He swallowed and held out his arm to the paramedic. "Start drawing my blood."

"What?"

"Do it," Carl ordered.

And while the woman leapt to follow the command in the alpha's voice, Mark finally hit pay dirt. "There!" he said, stabbing his finger at the tablet. Three guys tromping through the woods. One carried Julie. Bulky muscles straining. They'd get footprints for sure. Won't help much.

"What's that?" He fumbled to pause the screen. Why did his muscles feel thick and slow? Everyone peered around his finger. The smallest and youngest of the bastards. The guy had tossed his hoodie back to reveal a baseball cap turned backward on his head. The emblem on it showed up clear as day. "It's an A," he said, trying to figure out what the stylized letter meant. It had triangles down the left edge.

"Diamondbacks," Carl said. "Phoenix baseball team."

Mark frowned, his mind spinning through sports images.

Who the hell rooted for an Arizona team in Michigan?

"That's not much to go on," Tonya said. "But it's more than we had a minute ago."

Meanwhile, the paramedic was drawing his blood. She'd muttered something about it not being her specialty, but he hardly cared. And just when he was about to snap at her for the painful stab at the crook of his elbow, something else flashed on the screen.

With one arm restrained by the paramedic, he couldn't manage the video. Thankfully Tonya was there before him, steadying the tablet and the image. And there, slinking through the shadows, was a woman with short, sandy hair, long legs, and a grim expression.

Sour. Middle-aged. Bitter. Smooth carriage. Bitch. Shifter. "Who the hell is that?"

"Want to bet it's Theo's Crazy Cat Lady?" Tonya asked.

Carl rubbed his thumb down the screen. "Maybe. But I know her. I just can't remember where."

Mark jerked. "Figure it out!"

The explosion was meant for himself, not his alpha. Too much brain work. Too many thoughts. And zero control of the mental whirlwind. Thankfully, Carl didn't snap back at him. Meanwhile, the paramedic jerked Mark back to face her. For a little thing, she sure had some strength.

"Unless you want me to snap this needle off in your arm, you'll stay still."

"Who the hell are you?" he asked. Damn his grizzly nose for being off-line right now. He couldn't smell anything.

"Friend of Bryn's," Carl answered without really paying attention. His gaze was still on the screen.

Mark frowned at the woman. She was a wolf? Or just a normal in on the shifter secret? And why the hell did he care when Julie was with those bastards? Part of his brain was busy ticking off the seconds, counting up all the things those assholes could do while he was standing here with his thumb up his ass. It wasn't helpful and it sure as hell wasn't what he wanted to do. But at the moment, he was completely useless with his brain out of control. And in the middle of his frustration, a female voice interrupted his mental screaming. It was Julie's mother, her face tight with suppressed panic.

"Will someone please tell me what is going on? Where is Julie?"

Tonya moved smoothly to take hold of the woman's arm. Her voice was surprisingly gentle as she spoke. "I know this is upsetting, but please try to remain calm."

"Calm my ass!" snapped the professor as he pushed unsteadily to his feet. "I demand to know what the hell is going on. Where is my daughter?"

Tonya took a deep breath and began to explain things in an edited fashion. In the blink of an eye, she went from irritated no-nonsense police officer to sympathetic, calming influence. The tiny part of Mark's brain that was paying attention was impressed.

"She's a cat woman." Carl speaking. Who the hell was a cat? "Was she one of the cougars? From the wolf–cougar war?"

Oh. Bitch woman. Were the others cats? He hated the smell of cats. Made his nose twitch. They had Julie? Why?

Carl kept talking, his words slow as he searched through his memories. "Not one of the primaries, I think. Maybe support staff?"

Mark ground his back molars together. He wanted to bellow and yet no sound came out. He just hadn't the strength. Not with everything in his brain spinning at random. Another car coming up the lane. Police cruiser with the forensics guy Joey in the back. Everyone called him Mr. Science. Except his hair was more movie-star flowy. Where the hell was Julie? Gladwin wasn't large enough to have a full team. Mr. Science was shared with neighboring counties. Joey might find something they couldn't.

Julie!

"Mark! Go to the hospital," Carl snapped. An order. "There's nothing you can do here and a ton that can be figured out there."

Spinning out of control and so weak. Mark didn't have the focus to argue.

Carl gestured at the paramedic. "Make sure he gets full blood panels and the like."

She snorted. "Like anyone's going to listen to me."

He glared at her. "Use your nose. Figure out who's a shifter and tell them I said to do it. And if they need confirmation, then call me!"

She swallowed. "Got it, sir." Then she looked at Mark. "Please come with us."

Us? He frowned and looked around. There. Middle-aged partner leaning casually against the ambulance. *Move!* he ordered himself. *Quit being a lazy shit!* The man looked bored and a little bit pissed off.

"Ready for my help now?" the partner drawled.

"Chill," Mark snarled. Not a snarl. A weak almost-whisper. He recognized the guy as a longtime townie. He wasn't exactly in on the shifter secret, but he also wasn't completely ignorant. He probably knew that sometimes he just had to back away and not get involved. But that probably pissed him off. Why his mind was focused here was anybody's guess. But he took the moment of lucidity to grabbed for a joke rather than shove magic in the man's face. "I like pretty girls better than your ugly face."

The man grunted. "Same here." Then he opened the back door and gave a courtly gesture to invite Mark inside.

So weak. *Useless!* How the hell was he going to help Julie? "Carl…" he managed.

"Get your shit taken care of while I focus on mine," the alpha snapped. "I'll let you know as soon as we find an answer."

He had no excuse to argue, so he forced himself to nod. "Do it fast," he said, because…*Julie!* Because…no focus. *Because… what?*

Then he was inside the ambulance with the doors slamming shut. Trapped inside. Mind spinning. Where was Julie? What clue had he missed? Why the hell hadn't he saved her?

Chapter 16

Julie came awake slowly. It felt like swimming upward through cotton candy. Everything felt sticky sweet and left a foul taste in her brain. It made no sense, but that's what she was thinking as she finally got enough neurons on board to hear what her body was saying.

First off, it was saying, *Yuck.*

Second, *Ow.*

Third, *What the fuck am I lying on?*

Her face was cold and smooshed, her hip had a hot point of pain where it took the brunt of her weight, and her arm...*Oh, hell.* Her arm was numb. Getting the blood back into it was going to be a painful process.

She shifted, rolling awkwardly to her back. That made everything worse, but she forced herself to crack her eyes open.

It was dark, though not pitch black, thanks to a grimy window across the room. Metal bars surrounded her. Frantic, she scanned further and nearly freaked. She was in a cage with a small door padlocked on the outside. Panic tightened her throat.

Look further.

To her left was a long wood table covered with books, binders, and some computer equipment. To her right was a large furry lump. A really large furry lump. Her ears told her it was breathing fast and shallow. A steady rhythm, but not a healthy tempo. Whatever it was probably had a fever. It was in a cage, too.

Good. She wouldn't want to disturb the sleeping monster. Of course, she didn't want to be locked in beside a sleeping monster, either.

She started moving her fingers and toes, getting blood flow back. Then she noticed a dull Band-Aid at the crook of her elbow. Peeling back the covering, she saw that it covered an injection site.

Not good.

Nausea threatened to overwhelm her but she choked it a back. Every part of her felt clammy and sick. Was that a result of what they'd given her? Or was it just normal panic? Was there anything else wrong with her? She couldn't tell. It all ached, it was all terrifying, and she didn't know what the hell to do.

So she closed her eyes and tried to calm down. Unbidden, an image of Mark rose in her brain. She saw him kneeling before her, his heart in his eyes. The man was powerful. Not just physically and financially, but to the core of his soul. He was strong in ways that impressed the hell out of her. And in this image, he was kneeling before her laying all that power at her feet.

It was a memory, but a favorite one from a couple days before.

She'd been dozing on the couch and he'd been kneeling beside her, watching her sleep. When she'd opened her eyes, he'd given her this smile, half wistful, half lustful. It said as clear as day, "Take me. Take everything I have and love me."

She did.

She loved Mark.

And wasn't this a perfect time for that realization? When she couldn't grab the man and tell him, then make love with him until they dropped from exhaustion?

But panic had a way of crystallizing certain thoughts. And right now it really cemented the list of things she hadn't yet done in her life. She hadn't told Mark she loved him. She hadn't had children and watched them grow into fun people. And she hadn't mastered waterskiing, though why that was important, she hadn't a clue.

Well, then, she had plenty of reasons to get the hell out of this place. Or at least survive until Mark could come find her. That thought cheered her more than anything else because she knew for damn sure that Mark wouldn't stop until he ripped open the cage door and held her safe in his arms.

Unless Mark was dead. She remembered the pops, then hearing his grunt and the groceries falling.

No! She lost a full minute to the overwhelming despair of. No words, just a choking black fog of denial.

Her eyes went back to the furry lump. Was that Mark? She didn't think so, but how could she tell? The color seemed lighter, the size smaller, but in this gloom, how could she know? Hadn't Mark told her that the next time he shifted, he wouldn't be able to come back? Maybe that was him. Which meant the first step was to get him human again. So they could figure this out together.

"Mark?" she called softly. "Mark, is that you?"

She wanted to reach through the bars to touch him, but couldn't bring herself to risk that. Not until she was sure it was him. So she crouched next to the bars and called while searching for something to throw.

"Come on, honey. Wake up."

No response. And the floor was a simple concrete slab. Dirty with clods of dirt and hay, but not with anything large enough to throw.

Okay, try something else. She wasn't a helpless maiden who needed Mark to rescue her. She might not be GI Jane, but she could try some basic things. First things first. She tested every aspect of her cage. It was depressingly solid.

Weapons next. Anything?

Not that she could see. She peered through the gloom looking for exits, sharp things she could grab or make sharp by breaking, and anything else that a smart person could make into something useful. One exit to her left. Microscope and other science stuff on a far table. Everything out of reach. Not even a bit of water, and she was getting really thirsty.

Damn.

She was about to start screaming in frustration when door abruptly popped open. She looked up with hope only to flinch away from the sunlight. There was a person there. A man with wild hair and glasses. A few more blinks and she figured out he was wearing jeans and a dirty tee.

He flipped on the light, blinding her even further, then shut the door. He hummed quietly to himself—a Beatles song, she thought—as he pulled on a lab coat that had been hanging on a peg. Then he turned to her.

"You're awake," he said. "Good."

Now that her eyes had adjusted, she saw the man who had to be Evil Einstein. Mark had only mentioned him once, but the name had always struck her as funny. Not so much now that she was looking straight at him. Wild hair, middling frame, genial expression, but crazy eyes behind the glasses.

"Why am I here?" She quietly applauded herself for keeping her voice steady.

With the light on, she could see this was nothing more than a large shed. Concrete floor, wood walls, cheap roof. She tried to peer through the grimy window just to get a fix on where they were. Anything would help, but as far as she could see, it was dirty out there. "Because I need you," the man answered, his tone telling her she should have deduced that.

Fucker.

"For what?" Against her will, her eyes drifted to the furry lump. It wasn't Mark, she now saw. It didn't even fully look like a bear but a wrong combination of man and beast. The fur looked clumped and sparse, the joints and body proportions weird.

"For him," Evil Einstein answered as he went closer to the creature's cage. He frowned as he peered inside. "He's unstable."

Great.

"And you're going to help cement the shift."

"I am so not helping you."

He twisted, jerking his chin toward her arm. "You noticed the Band-Aid, right?"

She looked down, trying to ignore the itch she felt there. "What did you do to me?"

"Probably nothing. I gave you a small dose of what he had."

She jolted. "What?"

"It's to activate shifter DNA."

"I don't have any."

He snorted. "How would you know? I think that everyone has some of it. It's all a question of degree."

Oh, hell. "So you tested me? You think I can shift?" The idea intrigued her almost as much as it horrified her. She'd been experimented on in God only knew what way, which made her stomach roil with fear. But the idea that she could be like Mark? That she could shift to bear was appealing on a gut level.

He turned to stare at her. "Does it look like I have a gene sequencer here? Some way to map your DNA in minute detail? I don't even have an autosampler anymore."

"So you just injected me on the hope that it will work?"

He grinned at her, showing crooked teeth that were blindingly white. Freaky. "I injected you because I need more data. And because your only hope of survival is helping me."

The man wasn't making any sense. "I thought you said it probably wouldn't work on me."

"The first injection probably won't. Maybe it'll take three or seven. Or a hundred. I don't know, but I'm going to keep shoving it into your arm until I find a solution or you die. Either way I learn something."

Nausea choked her, but she held it back mostly because she wasn't sure where she was going hurl. There wasn't even a bucket nearby.

"By the way, he only took three injections to become this."

This was not good.

"Starting to see things my way yet?" he taunted.

Yes. No. Hell, she didn't know anything except she hated him. "What do you want me to do?"

"You and your father have been researching bonding rituals. You're a bit behind the ball on that. Elisabeth already told me about them, and she was able to stabilize the others. But this one is being stubborn." He kicked the other cage with a vicious curse. "So you're going to drink the potion, perform the ritual, and I'm going to see if it works."

"Why don't *you* perform it?" Not that she was averse to helping the sick bear-person next to her. At this point, her sympathy was all with him. But she had to delay as much as possible and hope that Mark found her. And any information was helpful, so she'd just keep him talking.

"Because he won't bond with me. I'm a guy, for one. And I've been experimenting on him."

Okay, so he had a good point.

"You, on the other hand, might just be what the grizzly needs. Plus, you'll be on your way to shifting anyway, so we'll hope that helps. Elisabeth says it does, so we'll go with that."

"You don't actually believe in magic potions, do you?"

He snorted as he leaned down into a small refrigerator she hadn't even noticed before. It was beneath the large table and he pulled up a familiar bottle. "Experiment 7" was written in bold letters in her father's hand.

"Of course not," he snapped as he held it out for her. "But there's science in the potions. And given what I've just done to your DNA, this just might work."

God, he was insane. "Exactly how much of this stuff have you shoved up your veins?" Was she going to go loony toons, too?

"None!" he said stiffly. "No point in activating myself until I have a way to survive it." Then his expression took on a wistfulness that was entirely too creepy. "I've got the bear DNA," he said. "Once I've perfected this process, I'll be able to shift. Finally."

This guy as a grizzly was not a good idea. But short of clocking him on the head, she had to survive anyway she could. Which meant she was going to bond with the poor bear captive because, at the moment, she didn't see any other choices. But then, she didn't have all the details yet.

"Exactly how do I do this?"

That's when freaky Einstein crossed to directly in front of her cage. He squatted down before her, his eyes narrowed, and his breath fouled the air between them with garlic.

"You don't know?" he asked.

"How the hell would I know?"

He looked to the side and the stack of books and things. A second glance now told her it was the material she and Mark had been studying. And those were her father's notebooks and probably his tablet. "You left the cabin. You went out to celebrate."

"We took a break," she said, her voice cold.

"You celebrated something. You were gone all night!"

They celebrated each other. They celebrated life. They celebrated falling in love, not that she'd thought to tell Mark that. "We didn't figure anything out. Ask Elizabeth for your answers."

"Her name's Elis*ssss*abeth," he said, lengthening the S. "She's very particular about that."

"Fine, ask Elis*sss*abeth."

He shook his head. "Can't. She's busy." He held out the bottle. "Chug-a-lug."

"You've got to be kidding me."

"Do I look like I'm joking?" he snapped as he pointed to the cage next to her. "He hasn't got much time left."

She stared at him, wondering if she understood what he wanted. "You've activated his bear DNA, but the shift is unstable. And somehow you think me drinking that shit will help."

He released a sigh that seemed to come from his toes. Like he was tired of explaining his nuttiness to people less smart. "It's very simple," he said. "I've activated his shifter DNA. I've started the process with yours. Thanks to your father, we've got the ingredients that force a chemical scent."

"The magic potion?"

He snorted. "Magic is simply something the ancients didn't understand. I do. Drink this and your skin will secrete a scent that should cause a reaction in his brain. Call them pheromones, if you must. You and he will sync like a baby syncs with its mother."

"Bonding," she said, finally understanding what he meant.

"Chemical reaction in the brain," he corrected. "But with measurable effects."

"You think it'll stabilize him."

He shrugged. "It's his only chance."

She stared at him, trying desperately to think of a way out of this. She came up with nothing.

"Or I could knock you unconscious and pour it down your throat," he said. "Though you might choke while I'm at it."

God help her, she considered it. But she couldn't do anything unconscious, so she took the bottle from his outstretched hand. Mark had said there wasn't anything poisonous in it. Just indigestion and killer BO. So with a sigh, she took a tentative sip. Not bad if you liked drinking clove and vinegar. *Ugh.*

"All of it. Now." There was no quarter in his expression. She really did believe that if she stalled any longer, he was going to find a way to knock her out.

Which meant she had to go for it. She plugged her nose and chugged, though the last bits were choked down more than swallowed. He grabbed the empty bottle from her hand while she was still gagging. Then he stood up with a pleased smile.

"Excellent. And while we're waiting for your scent to kick in, let's talk about your father's research. Why the hell would he put his own notes in code?"

She shrugged and tried not to retch. "It's shorthand."

"So translate it."

She looked at him, gratified that she'd guessed correctly before. But just to be sure, she asked the obvious question. "Is that why you attacked the cabin a few days ago? To get me to translate it?"

He rolled his eyes. "You might have noticed that those gentlemen were unstable as well." He glanced at the creature in the cage. "Though they did hold it together longer than him."

She held silent, watching his eyes. She'd never known a man yet who couldn't resist crowing about something he knew and others didn't. It only took a minute before he started talking again.

"Let me explain," he said, condescension in every syllable. "Elisabeth's immediate family was killed by the wolves, but she had relatives in Phoenix. Not full shifters, but with the cougar DNA. I developed the formula for activating it enough for them to partially shift. But it's unstable without her."

"Why? What's so special about her?"

"Exactly!" he crowed like she was a prize pupil. "She called it bonding. She held her relatives and sang to them. But I noticed the scent."

"So she has cougar pheromones that stabilized her kin."

He snorted. "Not enough. She brought twelve of her relatives to me for help. There are only four left now."

Good. The fewer insane baddies, the better.

"Whatever is stabilizing them isn't working as well. That's why we needed your father's recipes."

And her. To translate his notes.

"Thankfully, he had one bottle already made up. Convenient, don't you think?"

And stupid of her to pull it out and set it on the counter in full view of the baddies. "So why send them after me again?"

"I didn't send them anywhere. They were destabilizing. Elisabeth tried to bond with them, but it failed and they ran."

"They just ran? But..."

"They went back to the last thing they'd been ordered to do. The last time they were rational."

"My father's cabin." Well, Mark had said there was a kind of salmon instinct in the shifters. It's what kept the Gladwins right here in mid-Michigan. But she'd never thought it would apply the way he described.

Psycho Einstein shrugged. "Who can fathom the workings of an unstable mind?"

Sort of the pot calling the kettle black, right?

Meanwhile, he wiped his hands on a nearby towel as if touching the empty bottle had made him dirty. "I'm hungry. I think I'll get some lunch. Then I'll bring you a bucket, just in case." He flashed her a smile and a jaunty wave before disappearing out the door.

Julie stared after him, her thoughts whirling. But after a moment, they settled into two distinct sentences. *What the fuck? Please, Mark, find me soon.*

Chapter 17

Mark was flummoxed, and he was not a man to use a word like that. Baffled, gob-smacked, even discombobulated. Without his bear forcing a tighter focus, his brain spun off into a thousand different directions at once, none of them useful. Half of him was spinning into increased circles of panic about Julie. What was happening to her? Where was she? What could he do to help?

The other half of him was just spinning. Since adolescence, he'd daily longed for silence from his bear. Turned out, his bear was the grounded one in his brain. The grizzly focused on immediate things. If food and shelter were handled, the grizzly allowed another item on the list. Like finding Julie. But without the bear constantly limiting what could be dealt with, Mark ended up staring into space, lost in a thousand different thoughts. Sure, they were full, complete sentences, but they overlapped one another like layers of gauze a mile thick.

He couldn't function like this. Which is why he felt grateful for the time at the hospital. He did as he was told, followed simple instructions, and fought for control of a brain gone ADD.

It took him three hours. Three terrifying, horrendous, splintered hours. But thanks to a sympathetic nurse who let him slam back a pot of coffee, he managed to corral his thoughts into some form of order. First off, he had to get out of the hospital. Nothing he could do for Julie from here. So without overthinking it, he just put on his clothes and walked out. Then he got a cab and went straight to his alpha's house.

* * *

"What the fuck have you found out?" he demanded as he burst into Carl's home.

"Nothing more than I said in the last text ten minutes ago," Carl grumbled. He was sitting at his kitchen table looking haggard. Theo was nearby, looking as anxious as a broad-shouldered teen boy could. And Becca was doing what she always did when she was worried. She baked.

"Tell me again," Mark growled. And when Carl sent him a furious look, Mark remembered he was talking to his alpha. "Please."

Carl sighed and shoved his laptop away from him. "I remembered the Crazy Cat Lady. Her name is Elisabeth Oltheten and she was part of the cougar delegation way back when. But not a primary in it. Just someone who hung around helping. She got food for the cougars, made sure the hotels were set, and finalized transportation."

"So a secretary?"

"No. She wasn't allowed in the meetings. She was just around. I've reached out to the cats, which is how I got her name, but they don't know where she is."

"Or they aren't telling us."

Carl acknowledged that with a grimace. "She's some sort of respected elder." He pulled out his phone and started flipping it over and over in his hands. It was a nervous gesture that Mark understood. He was having trouble keeping his hands still too. "Tonya found out that she's got some relatives in Phoenix, Arizona, but that's about it."

"What does Alan think? Does he remember her?" As the two sons of the Gladwin alpha, both Carl and Alan had been at the peace talks so many years ago. But it was Carl who'd been the primary negotiator, showing signs of diplomacy well beyond his years. Alan had been there as secretary while their father had sat as the big bear who was going to keep the peace.

"Don't know," Carl growled. "He's not here."

Mark jolted, his gaze hopping to the stairway up to Alan's bedroom. "Why not? Where is he?"

Carl shrugged, his expression dark. Becca was the one who answered, her words tight and low. "He left almost a week ago, probably because of me."

Mark frowned, trying to rapidly sort through the possibilities in his brain. It didn't work well because there were too many. So he headed for the coffeepot while he grabbed the first idea that popped into his head. "You two fight?"

"No! We...Well...He might have thought we needed some space."

Oh. Right. Theo, Becca's adopted son, was part of the Gladwin Kids Camp (aka shifter school), which meant he slept in the cabins with the other teens. That left Carl and Becca, newly in love, alone here except for the third wheel named Alan. No wonder the guy made himself scarce.

"But it's not like him to stay gone. Not at a time like this."

"I know," grumbled Carl. "He sent me a text days ago saying he'd connected up with a law school friend and wouldn't be home for a while. Tonya says his phone is turned off."

Mark swallowed the coffee black, using the bitter taste to focus. What had Carl said? Phone. Off. "Turn it back on."

"It's off. It can't be—"

Mark grabbed Carl's laptop and started typing fast. With all the caffeine, his fingers flew on the keyboard. Meanwhile, the glare from his alpha had him confessing the truth. "So remember how Tonya put a GPS tracker on your truck ages back? Because you're the alpha and—"

"Yeah. I remember."

"Who do you think got her that really good tracker? And who do you think hacked your phones? She's good, but she's not a real techie."

Becca sighed, folding her arms across her chest. "Did you hack Carl's phone?"

Mark shrugged. "I may have installed a couple extra things on it. Like something that makes it *look* like it's turned off when it really isn't."

Carl stared at his phone like it had grown leper spots. "I can't believe you—"

Theo came off the couch, his teen eyes wide. "Did you hack Alan's phone? Can you teach me how?"

Becca gave the boy a stern look, but Mark barely noticed. "It's on your phone, too," he said to the boy as he continued to type. "See if you can find it."

"Awesome!"

It took Mark longer than he liked. This wasn't his computer and he had to maintain his thoughts for more than a few seconds. But it felt good to be doing something even if it wasn't disemboweling the bastards who had taken Julie.

"There you go. Here's where Alan's phone is." Then he frowned. What the hell was Alan doing near Twin Lakes? There was nothing up there but vacation rentals. "What do you know about this old law school friend?"

Carl stared at the screen, his expression tightening. "Absolutely nothing. What else can you do with that phone?"

Mark shrugged. "If the cops ask, absolutely nothing. But—"

"I'm your alpha."

Mark spun the laptop back toward him. "Then tell me what you want."

Becca put her hand on Carl's shoulder and Carl took hold of it. It was a casual, intimate gesture that made Mark's chest tighten. God, he hoped he'd be able to touch Julie again just like that. And a whole lot more.

Meanwhile, Theo piped up. "On TV, they turn on the phone. Make it into a microphone to hear—"

"Don't know if we'll hear anything, but I can give it a shot."
It took an embarrassingly long amount of time, but he got it to
work. And then he dialed the audio up to max while they all
strained to hear the tight, female voice.

Julie.

"He's unconscious. I don't care how much you threaten me, I
can't bond with an unconscious bear. I can't— Hey! Hey! Stop
it!" And then she screamed.

Chapter 18

Stop it!" Julie's screams did nothing to save her. Which really pissed her off and completely terrified her. At the moment, it was an even match between the two emotions, but she picked the one that got her motivated. Too bad it didn't matter.

No matter how angry she was, no matter how much adrenaline was pumping through her system, she could not stop her captors from pinning her down and injecting shit into her arm. They didn't even open the cage door but reached in and held her flush against the bars. She tried to fight, but she didn't have any maneuverability in the small space, and they were strong. Shifter strong, if she had to guess. And the one with the Diamondbacks ball cap on had freaky cat eyes.

"I'm cooperating," she screamed, even though she wasn't. "Don't do this! Don't!"

Too late. The crap went into her arm, and she felt the heat of whatever it was roll through her body like an evil wave. It was probably her imagination, but hell, even they didn't know what the compound was going to do to her.

They released her, and she scooted back as far as she could. Not more than eight inches, but it was enough for her rub her arm and glare at her captors. Not Elisssabeth, but Evil Einstein was here in all his manic glory. Plus his minions, one huge guy who said nothing and the freaky boy who kicked at her companion's cage whenever he could.

"Wake up, stinky!" the kid called.

"Leave him alone!" she shouted. It didn't help. The kid turned to grin at her, then kicked the bear's cage harder.

"Oops!" he said, mocking her with every breath. "Did I scare the dead bear?"

"He's not dead yet," she growled.

Evil Einstein pushed the boy aside. "But he will be. Soon. So if you're going to do something, you better get it done now."

"There isn't anything to do!"

Evil Einstein huffed out a breath. "You're already starting to stink. Even I can smell it."

Thanks a lot, bastard.

"Just talk to him. Try to bond." Then he glanced at the big henchman. "Put her in the cage with him. Maybe that'll help."

"No!" she cried out, ashamed that she didn't want to be locked in with her fellow captive. With light and time, she'd been able to make out more details. He was more like a lanky, furry man with paws, a big nose, and hair coming out of his ears. And he was just as much a victim as she was, but she still didn't want to climb into the same cage with him. "I, um…I can reach through the bars."

Einstein nodded, then gestured for the helpers to shove the cages closer together. They couldn't budge the other guy's, but hers slid easily enough. And then there was nothing stopping her from reaching through the bars to stroke the creature's furry leg.

The texture was coarse, the fur uneven. Was that ahead for her, too? Huge, knobby joints and oily fur? A fever she could feel radiating off the skin? Sympathy surged, bright and poignant. This was her future, and she would give what comfort to this creature that she could.

"It's okay," she said gently. "We'll figure this out."

His eyes opened, golden brown and sheened bright with pain. A quick stare, long and steady before fluttering shut. Enough time for her to realize that he was not only awake but smart enough to fake sleep. How much of his apparent illness was faked? Probably none of it, she thought with a grim kind of sadness. There was no way to simulate that shallow pant for as long as he had without it being real. And the mottled, thin patches of fur were definitely real.

"How much more time does he have?" she asked, already knowing that he would probably lie to her. Except the man rolled back on his heels and consulted a chart that was hanging on a nail on the wall.

"Hard to say," Evil Einstein responded. She'd already watched them take blood samples, temperature, and other readings on the guy. All while the creature was mercifully unconscious. Or so she'd thought. "The others died within a day of their fevers reaching one oh three." He tilted the clipboard to show her the marking. The last check listed his fever as 102.8.

Well, hell.

"And the ones who survived?"

He glanced at the two minions. "Elisabeth stabilized them long before then."

Right. "What's his name?"

The man shook his head, as if in disappointment. "He's Alan Carman. And he ought to have stabilized faster given that he's half shifter."

Carl's brother. *Shit.* She tried to remember him from that summer in high school, but all she got was an image of a gangly boy who had his nose in a book almost as much as she had. He was only three years younger than Carl and Mark, but at that age, it put him in middle school and completely beneath her notice. Though she did remember him offering her a sad smile one day from across a park. She'd been reading a mystery, and he had a legal thriller. And though they never spoke, he had crossed the entire field to sit at the same picnic bench as her and read. She remembered thinking that was nice of him even if he'd ducked his head back into his book every time she tried to speak to him. Pre-teens boys can be so dorky shy, but she held that image of him in her mind even as she spoke to the misshapen man he'd become.

"All right, Alan," she said as she squeezed his leg. "You probably don't remember me, but I remember you. You were nice as a kid. And wicked smart. So together, we've got enough brains to get through this, you and me. Okay, Alan? Okay?"

Then apparently the kid with the baseball cap got impatient. "Wake up!" he bellowed as he kicked the cage. Since Julie's arm was through the bars, it painfully jolted her arm and one of the edges dug deep.

"Watch it!" she snarled as she looked at the cut on her arm where the edge had cut into her. It wasn't deep, but it pissed her off. "We do not need that kind of help."

"Sure you do," the kid said, with a sneer. "Doc says blood is part of it. Maybe he should lick it."

She was about to tell him to go fuck himself, but decided Einstein was the better leverage point. "You want us to bond? Get teen nutcase the hell out of here."

Einstein sighed and gestured the kid back. And when the kid didn't move, stoic minion grabbed hold and jerked the teen back. Progress, she supposed. And then she looked back at Alan. The man's eyes were open. Golden brown and fever bright.

"Okay, Alan," she said with as much lightness in her voice as she could manage. "Let's do this, okay? And then when you're better, you can break open these bars and crack their heads like eggs, starting with junior, okay?"

His lips might have twitched. That might have been a smile. Or a mindless jerk of his facial muscles. She had no idea. But in this one thing, Einstein was right. They were out of time. So she settled against the bars and began to talk.

Chapter 19

Mark was in Tonya's squad car and speeding north within two minutes of hearing Julie's voice. Tonya sat beside him, coordinating with local law enforcement while Becca and Carl followed. Even with sirens and lights, it would take too damn long to get up there, but at least he could hear Julie's voice as she talked to Alan.

Jesus. They had Alan, too, and no one had even known.

Only one good thing came out of the drive. By the time they were within thirty miles of their destination, Mark's grizzly stretched, yawned, and came back to life with an audible growl. He didn't know if it was the adrenaline or just time for the drug to wear off. Either way, he was beyond grateful to have his normal body and brain back. Even if his grizzly hated being cooped up in a damned car with the siren piercing his ears. Meanwhile, Tonya shot him a dangerous look.

"You're back," she said.

He nodded.

"You're not going grizzly once we get there. Last thing we need is to put you down, too, because you can't shift back."

"I can't shift at all," he growled at her. That's why he'd convinced Carl to give him a pistol before they'd left. Without his grizzly, all he could do was glare really hard at people. Or punch them into the next county because even without grizzly strength, he was still a big guy. That would be satisfying, but it wouldn't be much help against a shotgun or their tranquilizer darts.

"Medical's on the way. Ambulance and a doc, all shifters." Her voice cracked a bit, but otherwise her gaze was on her gun as she slammed the clip back in.

"Good." He didn't want to think about what the bastards had done to Julie. He hadn't been able to tell from her screaming. Just that it had been awful and mercifully fast. Probably something medical, which terrified him even more. Because what the hell had they done to Alan that he needed a bond to stabilize?

"Can't you go any faster?" Tonya asked.

Not without killing innocent bystanders or wrecking the car. He didn't have his grizzly reflexes, and he was pushing the boundary of what he could do. And in the background, all he could hear was Julie pleading with Alan to stay calm. To hold on.

Her every word settled into his chest making it harder to breathe. The need to protect her was pounding behind his eyes, pulsing his vision and making him insane. Plus his mind still spun with horrible scenarios. What if he didn't get there in time? What if she died and she never knew how much he loved her? What if she thought she was alone?

Sweat made his hands slick. He glared at the dashboard GPS.

Thirteen minutes to destination. Jesus, all the things that could happen to her in thirteen fucking minutes. *Hold on!* He didn't know if he was talking to himself or her, but the words kept forming on his lips. *Hold on! Hold on!*

Then Tonya killed the sirens and suddenly the traffic thickened around him. Mark growled in fury, but Tonya was equally keyed up.

"We have to be quiet!" she snarled. "We can't risk them killing the hostages."

He didn't have the focus to respond. He was busy spinning around a corner. Ten minutes to destination.

Hold on!

The wheels spun again as he turned into vacation cabin suburbia. Large cabins around a lake, and every one filled with families. And then suddenly he saw a local PD car parked directly ahead.

He slammed on the brakes and was out of the car before the engine fully died down. Tonya carried the laptop that was still broadcasting Julie. He wanted to storm the place now, but Tonya shoved him backward with a curse.

"Wait! We're doing this smart," she snarled. He nodded, though it was a lie. No way was he waiting on anything. But he stayed in place long enough to get introduced to the cops and to hear the details of the plan. Search warrant obtained, and thanks to Google Maps and GPS, they knew exactly where she was—in some sort of backyard structure—but they still needed to keep the innocents out of the way. And not everyone had gotten here yet.

Enough. Mark started moving out, except he couldn't escape

Carl. Damn it. He hadn't even noticed the man arriving, but his alpha knew exactly what Mark intended and he held out a restraining arm.

Mark whipped. "Get the fuck—"

"Shut up and listen. I'm going with you, but we're doing it as men, got that?" He paused long enough to smile and wave nice and friendly at the cops. They didn't have jurisdiction here, not even Tonya, so it behooved everyone to play nice with the locals.

"I can't shift," Mark snapped, but even as he said the words, he wondered if it were true. His senses were perking up. He could smell the trees and the acrid scent of adrenaline wafting off everyone here.

"Get on a vest, then," Carl said. He hadn't put one on. A closer look showed him that Carl had on his tear-away stripper pants and a tee so thin it was nearly see through. That meant he was fully prepared to go grizzly and rip through his clothes if needed. By comparison, Mark was in what he'd been wearing at the hospital: dirty khakis and a hospital scrub for a shirt.

Bowing to necessity, he grabbed the vest Becca held out for him. He hated the weight and restriction, but he couldn't help Julie if he got shot. Then Tonya joined them, keeping her voice low as she jerked her chin toward the pair of local cops. "These guys don't know shit about shifters. They're going to freak if Alan's anything like the guys who attacked Julie's cabin. So go in, go fast, and get him out. Shifter ambulance and doc are already here, up that way around the bend." She pointed up the lane.

Mark nodded and headed out with Carl while Tonya and Becca distracted the cops. It wasn't the smartest way to handle this, but sometimes that's what happened when combining normal with the paranormal. Mark didn't care so long as it got him to Julie right away.

They slipped into the trees. There wasn't much coverage, but it would do for now. As far as he could tell, the bastards were relying on anonymity rather than real defenses. That was good, but he stayed on the alert and tried to keep his gun hand steady. He wasn't the best with a pistol, and he was twitchy from not being able to hear Julie's voice anymore. He hadn't realized how much reassurance he'd taken from her steady words. She was alive. She wasn't being attacked. But now that he couldn't hear her, he wanted to rip every building apart until he found her. Instead, he stuck to the shadows as he recruited all his senses.

Senses that were getting crisper by the second. About fucking time.

And then Julie started screaming.

Chapter 20

Alan was convulsing. Grand mal seizures that contorted his body and bent the bars of his cage. And there was absolutely nothing Julie could do about it but scream. Scream for bloody murder because no one was here to help him, and she was stuck in a damned cage.

They'd gone to dinner, damn it. Dinner! While Alan's body contorted and she was trapped, trapped, trapped! So she screamed out her desperation and prayed that someone would hear.

If only the bonding had worked. She certainly stank enough for whatever pheromones to permeate the space. Her body temperature had spiked, sweat and stink had made her light-headed, and maybe for a few moments there she had felt something. Fury, emptiness. Connection? She didn't know, and for the first time in her life she *hated*. She despised Evil Einstein to a degree she'd never believed she was capable. While she spoke soothing words to Alan, she stewed in fantasies of ripping them apart. Of dancing while their lifeblood poured into the ground from painful, gut-wrenching wounds.

And then Alan had started to convulse and she had nothing in her but her screams.

The door burst open and a large form entered, gun drawn and eyes narrowed. Her subconscious recognized him long before her brain got the message. Her scream choked off into a sob of relief even as her eyes outlined a large body with unkempt hair, as if he'd been pulling at it in worry.

Mark.

He was at her cage a moment later, grabbing the lock, even as he turned to see Alan. It was a pause between seizures, and like the other two times, Julie prayed that it would be the end. That he'd breathe easier and rest. But just like before, four seconds ticked by in quiet before the convulsions began on the fifth.

"Help him!" she cried.

Carl leapt into the room in that moment, gun also drawn but he went straight to Alan's cage. Then he tossed his weapon to Mark before shifting into full grizzly. There was a quick shimmer and then a huge grizzly with a silver streak down his back crowded everything else in the room. A single swipe of his paw shredded Alan's cage. Another took out Julie's lock. She started to scramble out, but her legs were startlingly weak. Not a problem, though, as Mark hauled her out, wrapping her firmly in one arm while the other snapped open the buckles on his vest.

As soon as he was able, he hauled her to his mouth in a quick kiss. She wrapped herself around him, sobbing out her terror even as he set her apart from him.

"Put this on!" he ordered as he shoved his vest at her. She didn't want to take it and leave him exposed, but he didn't give her any choice. He dropped the thing in her hand and turned to get a grip on Alan. It's not like Carl could do it in his grizzly form.

Except that there was little room to maneuver in this tiny space. Julie had to climb on top of her ruined cage and pull on the vest simply to get it out of her hands. Then—thank God—Alan's seizure stopped. His body collapsed into a boneless heap, and he didn't seem to breathe. Julie held her breath even as she buckled on the vest, counting the seconds and praying. But Mark wasn't wasting a second. He started hauling the large man out of the cage the moment he could get a secure grip.

And then they ran out of time.

The little shit minion came in first with his ball cap askew and his mouth pulled into a wide grin. If she hadn't been looking at just the right way, she wouldn't have seen what he did. One second he was running in, popping the buckle on his too big denim shorts. The next second he was leaping out of them as he shifted into a beige cougar wearing a band tee. His ball cap flew off, and his shorts dropped to the ground, but what Julie saw most was the long sharp points of his claws.

Julie screamed, unable to give any more warning than that. The problem was that grizzly Carl was facing into the shed and there was no room to maneuver around. Which meant the cat landed on Carl's back and dug in.

Carl roared and reared up, forcing everyone else to flatten

backward—Julie against the wall and Mark, with Alan in his arms, scrambled onto the table that had held the research books. The damned cat clung to Carl's back, and Julie smelled blood, but Carl wasn't fighting in a blind rage. He was backing up, slamming the creature against the table and wall as he headed toward the door. Except the other henchman was in the door now, though he, too, pulled back at the sight of bear and cat battling in this small space. And behind him stood Evil Einstein with his mouth ajar.

"Julie!" Mark cried. "Grab the gun!" He had shifted Alan so that the man hung limply over his shoulder and was doing his best to step forward toward the door without interfering with the Carl–cat battle. Julie spied a pistol sticking out of the waistband of his khakis and fumbled forward to grab it. Now wasn't the time to tell him she sucked as a marksman. But she at least knew the basics. Not that it was easy holding the weapon steady as she thumbed off the safety.

Bang! Bang!

At first she'd thought she'd accidentally fired, but it hadn't been her gun. It was Stoic Minion as he elbowed aside Evil Einstein while firing his pistol. One shot must have hit Carl because the grizzly roared in pain and redoubled his efforts to throw the cat off his back. The other went wide, making a hole in the side of the shed much too close to Mark's head.

The sight triggered all the furious hate that had been boiling inside her. These bastards needed to die. Carl and Mark were busy, and so it was up to her. She had a gun, and the bad guys were within a few feet of her. But there were many pounds of roaring, twisting, slamming grizzly–cougar in between her and them.

Which is when she saw her moment. Carl slammed his back hard against the wood table, the microscope and vials shattering from the impact. His head arched back and she feared he'd just cut himself in two when she realized that had been the point. The cougar on his neck had slipped lower, down to his hips while his claws ripped long, bloody streaks in the grizzly's fur. It was the cat who broke, not the bear. And as the creature whimpered and fell, nothing was between her and Stoic Minion but the open door.

Time for Julie to run outside shooting.

Stoic Minion had his gun up, but he was aiming at Carl whose front was now exposed. Julie did two things at once. She ran forward and started shooting. No aim, just a rapid pulling of the trigger with the muzzle aimed ahead of her.

Bam bam bam!

The gun bucked wildly in her hand, but she watched with gleeful satisfaction as Stoic Minion jerked and the hand carrying his pistol went wide. Red sprouted on his chest, but she barely registered it. She was rushing outside and seeing Evil Einstein running for his life toward the trees.

She took off after him with no clear plan. She just knew that he was the one with the medical knowledge. He knew what shit he'd injected into them. Any hope of saving Alan would require him alive. Though she had no problem with maiming the guy.

"Julie! Stay with the cops!"

Julie slowed down at Mark's voice, not because of what he said but to wait for him. He was slower, burdened as he was with Alan, and it was her job to protect him as much as she could. He and Carl made it to her side quickly, and she pointed into the woods.

"Einstein went that way. We need him!"

Grizzly Carl took off. God, bears were fast. Mark was running but with Alan still whipped over his shoulder, he was a good deal slower.

"Stay with the cops!" Mark snapped as he kept running, but not in the same direction as Carl.

Cops? What cops? Oh shit, those cops bursting through the house with their guns drawn. She recognized Tonya but the other two looked scary as hell. She threw her hands up in the air, but she didn't stop running. Every part of her wanted away from that damned shed.

"Stop! Police!" one of them bellowed, and he was aiming at Mark.

Oh fuck! "No!" she screamed, stumbling as she tried to block their view of him. Oh God. All she could see were the muzzles aimed right at Mark. "He's rescuing us!"

"Don't shoot!" barked Tonya, her voice loud with command. But it didn't seem like the other two were listening. "He's taking Alan to the doc!"

Really? That was good. And why had her knees just given out?

"Where's Carl?" Tonya barked, the tone so forceful that Julie answered even as she fell to the ground.

"That way." She jerked her hand in the direction of the words. "After Einstein."

Tonya nodded and ran off, bellowing her command over her shoulder. "Stay here!"

Julie didn't know if the order was for the other cops or for her. Either way, she wasn't going anywhere. Her entire body was shaking. *Where is Mark?* The other cops advanced on her, their eyes scanning everything.

"Don't do it!" one of the cops bellowed.

Julie's heart leapt to her throat. She wasn't doing anything, but her voice had frozen.

"Put it down now!" the other cop ordered.

Unwillingly, her gaze jerked to the nearest cop. It was only then that she realized he wasn't pointing his gun at her but at the shed. She turned—slowly—to see ball cap kid on the floor of the shed. He was lying on his stomach, a pistol braced on the concrete as he aimed at her.

Oh shit.

"Bitch," he said. Then she heard the bang of a gun and she face planted. No pain, just suddenly, the world slapped her in the face. Had she been shot? All she knew was that her vision was blurry as she blinked grass from her eyes.

Gunshots pounded against her eardrums. If she'd been able to move, she would have covered her ears. As it was, she just lay facedown and prayed everyone thought she was dead. And in her head, one words echoed over and over in her brain.

Mark. Mark. Mark.

"Are you all right? Miss? Miss!"

A rough hand pulled at her, and she cried out in pain. "Let go!"

She jerked her arm back and then winced as the burn built. Damn it, her arm was on fire. Shit. She'd been shot. A long hot red streak across her upper arm. "Ow!" she said, putting all her anger into that one word. "That bastard shot me!"

She turned to look and then wished she hadn't. Ball cap boy was dead. Really, really dead.

But wherever he was, stoic guy wasn't far behind. "Where's the other one?" she asked, scanning the ground in panic.

"The other one?"

"Yeah." She took a breath, trying to remember. She'd shot him, right? She couldn't even remember. "The bigger one." He wasn't anywhere she could see. Then she saw a patch of grass that had slick dark blood on it. *Take that, you bastard.* Though a second later she started to worry. *Where the hell is he?*

Meanwhile, the cop who'd grabbed her arm talked into a shoulder mic, something about, female hostage recovered, but she couldn't focus on his words. Her mind was starting to catch up with her, and every part of her was looking for Mark.

Was he okay? He'd taken Alan to the ambulance, but she didn't see them. And she desperately needed to see him just to reassure herself that he was alive. That she was alive. That everything was finally, absolutely okay.

"It's just a graze, but there's an ambulance nearby. Do you think you can walk?" the cop asked.

"I..." She swallowed, forcibly pulling her thoughts together. "I'm fine." No, she wasn't, but she didn't want him fussing over her. She needed to find Mark.

"You're doing great," he said with a reassuring smile, as he looked hard at her wound. It wasn't even really bleeding hard. She'd gotten worse that first time she'd Rollerbladed, but damn it stung.

Then he helped her stand and gestured around a large vacation house. Now that she was out of the shed, she was getting a pretty good idea that she was somewhere in Michigan at a summer home around a lake. They walked together with the cop keeping a wary eye out. But once they made it to the front yard, she saw and heard the ambulance driving rapidly down the road. *Away from them.* The cop cursed, but Julie's eyes were on Mark. He'd been watching the vehicle pull away, but as it tore down the road, he turned around.

She knew the moment he spotted her because his body suddenly sagged in relief. She laughed, the sound more sob of relief than humor. He looked exhausted and worried and handsome in his scrub shirt and dirty khakis. Nothing about him was clean or crisp, and yet he'd never appeared more perfect to her.

She called out his name and ran straight for him. If the cop tried to stop her, she didn't notice. And within a second, she was in his arms. He held her tight, lifting her up as he squeezed her, and everything inside her felt *right.* She felt him bury his face in her hair and one of them shuddered in reaction, though she couldn't tell who.

"I knew you'd come," she said against his shoulder. "I knew it."

He didn't speak, just squeezed her tighter. At some point the cop interrupted them. He might have been speaking for a while. She didn't know and didn't care. But eventually the words penetrated. Or more specifically, Mark's reaction to the words.

"She's been shot. She needs a doctor."

Mark tensed and rapidly set her back on her heels. His hands started patting her body while his gaze raked her from head to toe.

"It's a scrape," she said. "I'll be fine."

"You're going to the hospital—" he began, but the cop cut him off.

"You're going to stay out of this. If you hadn't run in there half-cocked, this would have been a lot safer. And the assholes wouldn't be halfway to Canada by now."

Julie watched as Mark visibly controlled his expression. He clearly wanted to rip the guy's head off, but she set a hand on his chest. She felt the heat of him and the uneven stutter of his breath. He wrapped his own hand around hers, and together they both seemed to breathe easier. "You're right," he finally said. "But she was screaming. I couldn't—" His voice choked off.

"I'm fine," Julie said. "And Alan's going to be fine." She looked down the road. "That's where the ambulance went, right?"

He nodded. "He stopped seizing, but he looked pretty bad." Then he looked back to the cop. "I can take her to the hospital. She's safe with me, I swear. And you can go back…" He gestured with his chin.

"My partner's still searching." The cop clearly wanted to go help, but didn't like leaving her alone.

"Mark can take me to the hospital," she said. "You go help."

"I can call for another ambulance."

Julie smiled at the man. "No. Please. I'm safe now."

The guy glared at Mark, but in the end he gave in. It helped that another squad car was coming down the road. "I'll find you at the hospital," he said then he started jogging back around, speaking into his mic and calling for his partner's twenty.

Julie took a breath, then wrapped herself in Mark's arms again. He was strong and solid, he held her close. She was safe. Finally, she was safe

"Thank you," she whispered.

"I'd die if something happened to you," he said.

She pinched him where she gripped his side. "Stop talking about dying," she said. "I hate it."

He didn't answer, just pressed a tender kiss to her forehead. And then another to her cheek. And before long, she had lifted her face to his and they were kissing deeply. But it wasn't rough or even rushed. It was heartbreakingly tender as he took care with her lips, her mouth, her tongue. Every second felt reverential, and she melted into him until in her mind, they were one.

Then he pulled back. "I need to get you to a doctor," he said against her temple.

"Okay," she said. And they turned as one, walking to a truck. "It's Carl's," he said as he pulled out the key. Behind them, the new squad car pulled in and officers got out but didn't bother them. Must not have seen them, she realized because the truck was parked on the opposite side, half hidden in the woods. In fact, it was shoved up so close to the trees that it was going to be hard to open the passenger side door.

"Do you need to help Tonya or Carl?" she asked, looking over his shoulder as the new police officers ran around the house.

He shook his head. "I'm not leaving you. Besides, I can't shift. Or I shouldn't. And I'm shit with a gun." There was worry in his voice, and she shared his anxiety. Even so, she was grateful that he chose to stay with her. She still felt shaky and the world had a brittle quality to it just then. She didn't even want to let go of him to climb into the truck.

He seemed to understand that—or maybe needed to hold her as much as she needed it—so he pulled open the passenger door but didn't push her in. They just held each other. One breath. A thousand breaths. It didn't matter. She wasn't ever letting him go.

And then they ran out of time.

Chapter 21

Mark heard the sound first. A low growl that had his hair sticking up and his body tightening with adrenaline. A furious animal was nearby. A cat predator, by the sound of it, and ready to attack.

"Get in the truck," he ordered, shoving Julie inside.

She went awkwardly, startled enough to gasp out a "What?"

He didn't have time to answer. He spun around and saw the creature stalking around a tree trunk. A cougar. A shifter by the feel of her, strong in magic, older in chronological age. But in shifters, age often meant they were harder to kill, not easier. Magic or DNA strengthened the body and strong emotions sometimes made them downright invulnerable.

And he was standing here as a human without a weapon.

He knew better than to dash around the truck. Any movement and she'd be on him. The way her tail was twitching told him that much. But the growl was what terrified him. She was in the grips of fury, dark and ugly. The best he could hope for was to talk her down, but he doubted it would work. Especially since her eyes fixed equally on him and Julie. She wanted them both. She was just deciding which one she would take out first.

Which left him with a second option. A bad one, but it was that or watch her rip through the truck for Julie.

He unbuttoned his khakis and toed off his shoes. Sometime in the last adrenaline-fueled fight, his grizzly had finally come out of hibernation. He probably had the ability to shift now, but doing it in clothes would hurt. Behind him, Julie had finally figured out what was going on.

"Get in the truck!" she screamed.

Bad choice. The cougar hunched lower, jaw clicking as she took a slow step around a tree for a better angle. Mark made a quick gesture behind his back, hoping Julie saw it and understood it meant she was supposed to be quiet.

"You're the cat woman," he said calmly. "Elisabeth Oltheten." The bitch who was working with Evil Einstein to kidnap Julie and experiment on her, not to mention Alan, Theo, and some werewolf cubs. And that just made his blood burn. Which in turn was the last trigger he needed.

His grizzly took charge, itching like needle pricks beneath his skin. He wanted to meet the bitch and fight tooth and claw. He wanted to rip her apart as only a grizzly could. But even as he stepped out of his shoes, he heard Julie behind him.

"Don't you dare!" she cried. "Get in the truck!"

He couldn't. No way was the cougar going to let him move that far.

"Stay calm," he said to everyone there, himself included. "Let's think this through. Elisabeth, if you attack, I'm going to rip you apart. You know I can—"

She leapt.

No pause, no hesitation, no reason behind it. She attacked. He shifted. There was no choice.

He met her on the upload. That's what he called the shift into grizzly. His bear was larger and taller than he was, so when he changed, his body grew upward, outward, and in this case—straight into her claws at a speed even a cougar couldn't beat.

Somewhere in the back of his mind, he heard Julie scream. It fired his blood, reminding the grizzly that he was fighting for his mate. He would protect her no matter what.

He was hampered by his clothes, but he tore through them. And in that time, the cougar clamped her jaws on his shoulder. Pain ripped through his mind while his legs finally got free. She bit down like a vise, holding herself in place so her back claws could rake down his chest and belly. He grabbed at her while a roar tore through his throat.

Then he let his brain step fully back so that instinct could fight unimpaired. His last logical thought was that he had to use his superior strength to rip her off his body and throw her as hard as possible against the nearest tree.

Then it was only teeth. Claws. Pain.

Bite until he tasted blood. Contract muscles. Squeeze.

Her back claws dug into his gut. His claws gripped her body and wrenched. She wriggled in his hold. Her head lifted from his shoulder, aimed for his neck. In that split second before she bit, he threw her away. He heard her impact against a tree, the thud followed by a whimper of pain. He fell forward, dropping to all fours while his belly cramped and bled. He could smell his own life draining to the ground, but his eyes were on her.

She rolled to her feet with a snarl. He roared back, gathered himself, pushed upward into a stand. He would kill her now, but she leapt away. She was fast and smart.

He pursued. Into the woods. Rage burned through his being. Too slow. She was gone.

Gone.

He dropped onto all fours, anguish radiating through his shoulder. He flinched and fell to the dirt. His belly flooded his mind with fire.

He roared again. *Anger. Destroy. Kill.*

And over all of it: *Pain.*

He had to return to his mate. He had to protect her. But most of all, he had to hide himself and her until he healed.

He lumbered around, searching behind him only to realize she wasn't there. Her scent was there, but he saw no grizzly. Only a human, pink and unimportant, though something about it made him pause. Mate? He knew the citrus smell of her, acrid with fear, but this pink creature wasn't his mate. And yet his nose twitched with interest. Important. He inhaled hard, trying to focus.

Pain.

Injured.

His thoughts scattered. Priorities realigned. His mate was gone. He had to hide and heal.

He roared one last time, the statement filled with all the mournful fury that coursed through him. He would leave, he decided. He would find a den to hide in and heal, and then he would search for her again.

He was still twitchy with pain and fury. He wanted that bitch cat. He wanted his mate. He wanted to kill something and end the pain. And then, in the midst of this disconnected anger, one of the humans annoyed him.

Chapter 22

M^{ark, come back!"}

Damn it! The stupid grizzly man wasn't listening. It had been hell watching cougar and bear fight. She'd been helpless, doing her best just to scramble through the woods following the fight. But now the bitch was gone and Mark was hurt. He needed help, but he wasn't listening to her. Thankfully, he wasn't moving fast, so she took a deep breath and did what she'd do with a frightened dog. A really big dog.

She lurched forward and grabbed the scruff of his neck.

"Mark! Pay attention!"

Bad idea! The creature lurched, tossing his head at her. Pain exploded across her ribs as she went tumbling backward. *Stupid, stupid.* But at least she'd gotten its attention. That was good, right?

The grizzly lumbered toward her, his nose twitching as his belly dripped blood on the ground.

"You have to shift back," she said, every word a painful push of breath. But she had to get through to the man. "You have to become human." She knew enough about the size differential now to realize that if he turned back into a man, most of his wounds would shrink and heal.

A hard female voice sounded behind her. "Back away, Julie. Slowly."

It was Tonya, and she turned to see the officer standing carefully behind a tree trunk with her gun drawn.

"Don't shoot!" Julie called in panic. "That's Mark!"

Tonya's expression flattened into a dispassionate stare. "I know who it is. I'd recognize that roar from a mile away. Why do you think I'm here? Now move away."

Julie did move. She pushed to her feet right into the firing line. "I'm not going to let you shoot him."

The woman cursed and moved to the other side of the tree. "He's feral, Julie. You have to accept that the Mark you knew is gone."

"Bullshit. He just has to change back."

"He's not going to. Can't you feel it?" Then she answered her own question. "Of course you can't, but I can. He's an animal now, nothing more, nothing less."

Julie refused to believe that even though she knew it was possible. "He'll come back to me. You'll see." Tonya opened her mouth to argue, but Julie stepped in front of her again. "And even if he doesn't, there's no reason to kill him."

Tonya sighed, aiming her gun down. "Do you think I want to do this? I grew up with him! But ferals go crazy, and when they do, they hurt people." She took a breath. "Mark doesn't want that. And he asked me to do this, Julie. He made me promise."

Julie was close enough to see Tonya's face. The sheen of tears was unmistakable. Oh, hell. Tonya wasn't being cold or heartless. It was the mask she wore when she was doing something impossibly hard. Like killing a childhood friend because he'd pleaded her to do it.

But even knowing that, Julie couldn't let her do it. "I can bring him back. Look," she said, pointing to where Mark had dropped to the ground. "He's waiting for me. He's safe."

"He's hurt," Tonya snapped. "And that makes him dangerous."

"He won't hurt me," she said, praying it was true. So she focused back on her love, taking a single step closer to him. "Hey, Mark. It's time to get back to being human. Come on."

"Not too close!" Tonya growled, low in her throat.

Mark turned toward the sound, his nose twitching as he smelled the environment.

"That's right. It's me," Julie said. "It's me."

He pushed back up and started moving forward, but not toward either of them. He lumbered past them toward the truck, his steps heavy and slow. Julie looked to the blood that had pooled where he'd dropped. There was a gory mess there, telling her that he was bleeding steadily. Exactly how serious were his wounds? How much blood loss could a grizzly sustain?

"Hey, Mark. You really need to shift back. It's important. You need to be human."

He didn't pay any attention to her. And as he plodded to the truck, Tonya managed to site him again with her gun.

"You need to give him up, Julie," she said, her voice so brittle every word cracked. "We've known this was coming for years."

"Not yet," Julie insisted. She followed Mark, racking her brains for a way to reach him. She'd barely gotten within a dozen feet of him when he abruptly roared. It was an anguished sound, filled with an aching loneliness that made her vision blur with tears. "I'm here, Mark," she said. "Come back to me."

He turned toward her, his head swinging slowly. She smiled at him. Now was when—

He shifted away from her. It took her another few moments to realize he was leaving. Just…leaving.

"No," she whispered. Understanding burst through her consciousness, more painful than anything. This wasn't Mark. Mark wouldn't leave her. Mark loved her. She knew that from the depths of her soul. So if the grizzly was walking away, then it couldn't be Mark. It couldn't be the man she loved.

She stumbled, the agony in her heart making her cry out. "Please, Mark, look at me. You have to look at me." He stopped, then swung his head around until he stared right at her. Liquid brown eyes that narrowed as he focused. From the corner of her eye, she saw Tonya dash a hand at her eyes, wiping the tears away. But her gun hand held steady where it aimed right between the bear's eyes.

"Not yet, Tonya," she sobbed. "Not yet." Not with the grizzly looking at her so intensely, his nostrils flaring as he sniffed. Then he curled his lips back and a low growl vibrated through the air, loud enough that it was a physical sensation against her body.

God, she must reek. The thought was a random one, a flit of

information through her terrified brain. She didn't want to be mauled by an angry grizzly, but she couldn't give up the hope that Mark was still in there.

Wait. Reek.

She did reek. From whatever was in that stupid potion she'd drank. And the crap they'd shoved into her arm. Could this be the bonding? Could her scent be right now releasing some sort of chemical whatever into his brain?

It was a slim hope, but all she had. So with a shaking hand, she raised up her arm. Her heart was slamming hard in her chest, too many emotions choking her. But she still did it. She still held out her hand straight at his really big mouth and tried to speak without stammering.

"That's right, Mark. Smell me. It's Julie. You remember me, right?"

The grizzly leaned forward, his nose flaring and narrowing as he breathed. The hot air curled about her wrist, and Julie wanted to close her eyes. She didn't want to see if she was about to lose a hand. She didn't want herself die. But she couldn't look away. She was mesmerized by the flare of his nose. The heat of his breath. And the long dart of his pink tongue.

What?

He was licking her hand.

Wet and hot, the scrape of his tongue made her tremble. Was this good? She didn't even know. But he wasn't eating her. So she just started talking, words flowing as she tried to connect any way she could. "I love you, Mark. It's crazy, I know, but it's true. I love that you are so strong. Not just physically, but in spirit.

Your mind is disciplined, your focus perfect, but it's your heart that caught me. You look out for people. Tonya told me that you drop everything to protect kids. That you've donated a lot of your money to scholarship funds for the Gladwin bears."

He stopped licking her hand. They were face-to-face now. She was kneeling on the ground, and he was facing her, his nostrils flaring as he took another step forward. She could smell his blood now, even heard the plops as it dripped onto the scattered leaves beneath them. If he attacked, she'd be dead in a second. No way was Tonya's pistol going to do anything before he ripped out her throat. But even so, Julie remained still as he scented up her arm to her neck. God, she was letting a grizzly next to her throat. She closed her eyes rather than look into his mouth and the sharp points of his teeth. She heard him sniff her and shook when a rumble came from deep inside his throat. But this was Mark. And if he was going to bond with her, then she had to feel safe with him. She had to relax and believe. So she started talking again, her words as much for herself as him.

"Did you know that you make me feel safe? Even when I'm terrified, I feel better when I'm with you. Even when you're growling like that."

The rumble continued, the sound was low and angry. A purr gone bad. Her breath choked her. It took a dozen rapid heartbeats before she could speak again.

"I love that you make me feel beautiful. No one has ever looked at me like you do. You make me beautiful, Mark."

He opened his mouth. She could feel his jaw widen. The heat was intense, and she shivered. And then…

He licked her. A soft, tentative caress of his tongue.

Without thought, she let her head drop back. She bared her throat to him, and she felt him lick her. Once. Twice. Wet and sloppy, and she chuckled.

Bonded. They were bonded.

She put up her hands to touch his face. Fur, muzzle, wet nose. She chuckled as she pulled them apart enough so that she could look into his eyes.

Liquid brown. But this close, she could see the flecks of gold. And then *more*. She felt magic.

She watched as Mark twitched, jerking his head to her and baring his teeth. He was getting anxious and that wasn't good. But something was happening to them. Something was happening to *her*. Over his shoulder, Tonya cursed but Julie didn't have the ability to warn her off. She couldn't speak at all.

Meanwhile, Mark was backing away. His eyes had gone frantic and his lips were curled back. Suddenly he reared upward while she tried to scream.

She heard the rapport of Tonya's gun. Three rapid shots. If they hit Mark, there was no sign of it amidst his bellowing. Then Julie's body seemed ripped from her. Her back arched, her hands expanded, and her face. Holy shit, her face was on fire.

She screamed as her entire body seemed to explode. Her teeth scraped her tongue. And her skin burned while her body flung wide with hairy arms and extended claws. And the loose bullet-proof jacket choked her enough that she ripped at it with hands gone thick and uncoordinated.

She had no understanding of what happened. She knew pain

and power as the grizzly in front of her wrapped his arms around her. They were grappling, and she was nearly his size. Lord, she was pissed, and she roared as loud as she could right in his face.

A bear, she realized, though dimly in the back corner of her thoughts. She was a freaking grizzly bear. Except when she looked at herself, she was not full bear. The fur was patchy and uneven, her hands were huge and her joints thick, but not quite paws, though not really human either.

And then she lost thought as he gripped at her. Another bear—her mate—clawing at her sides.

She fought because she was frightened. She bit at him and swiped at his nose. He was bigger and stronger as he pushed at her. She fell to all fours and roared in fury.

He wanted to mount her, but she wasn't ready. Not yet.

But soon.

She growled, baring her teeth, and he backed away. She smelled his blood and worried at the scent. And when he dropped down to all fours, she paused, sniffing the air as she focused on his injuries. Blood, seeping slowly onto his fur. Pain that needed to be soothed.

She nudged forward with a low grumble. He responded with a dull moan. Her mate was in pain. She nudged his shoulder, nipping and licking at it as he thumped to the ground before her. Then gently, ponderously slow, he flopped back onto his side, exposing his raw belly.

She eased his pain. She licked his shoulder and then his belly. Tasted his blood in her mouth and knew that this was the way to healing.

She was still licking him when he shimmered. Tiny electric bolts of power hit her tongue, causing her to recoil. But the magic held them both together. When he trembled, she did as well. Their brown fur faded, replaced by pink skin. Bones contracted, muscles twitched and realigned.

Unsteady, she wobbled on her knees, her palms feeling cut by the underbrush. Below her, Mark's naked body shivered, and his eyes blinked in a dazed pain.

Human. He was human, she realized. As was she.

His gaze caught hers. His eyes widened in shock, but then immediately softened. He smiled at her while she gaped at him. What the hell had just happened?

She tried to speak, but her mind was too fuzzy to hold on to words. She tried to move, but there was no strength in her body. So she wobbled and dropped face-first into his chest. His arms wrapped around her, strong and vital. He held her secure while her eyes fluttered shut and the darkness overwhelmed her. But even so, she had the strength to hear sound and understand its meaning.

"Julie," he said. "My mate."

Chapter 23

Three days.

Three fucking days, and she still hadn't woken up.

Mark stared at Julie's still body, counting the steady rise and fall of her chest. She was breathing. Her heart was beating. And most important, this was all completely normal after a first shift. New shifters sometimes slept for a week after their first change. Three days was average. Except nothing about what had happened to her was average.

She had bonded with him, thereby saving his life and his sanity. Somehow, she'd connected them and that had bled off enough bear so that he could think. Instead of being all consuming, the grizzly in him had settled, sharing space in his brain like never before. And from that place, he'd been able to come back to human.

A miracle for him, but for her? She'd been overwhelmed. She'd shifted but not been able to maintain the form. And now she was lying unconscious in a hospital room because of what she'd done to save him.

"This is normal, Mark. Quit beating yourself up."

Mark looked up as Carl entered the hospital room. He was looking tired, but in a good way. As if the statesmanship of being their alpha was easier somehow. Becca's doing, obviously, and Mark was happy for the man, but that didn't ease his worry about Julie.

"How are you feeling?" Carl asked.

"Fine."

"Have you slept?"

"Sure." There was a cushioned chair to the side, and Mark had caught some Zs when Julie's mother and sister had been with her. Right now they were picking up the professor from the cabin so he could visit as well, which gave Mark a chance to sit on the edge of her bed and hold her hand. Her still, too hot hand.

Did she have a fever?

He glanced at the monitor and saw that her temperature was 99.4, aka shifter normal. But she wasn't a shifter. Four days ago she'd been 100 percent human with a 98.6 degree body temperature. He knew because he'd touched every inch of her body. He'd slept with her tucked up beside him. And he had wrapped her against him every moment he could. He knew what her temperature was, and this was hot for her. Unless it was the new norm. Unless she had been permanently changed in an amazing way.

But he didn't dare hope for that. Not the way his luck usually ran.

"Come on, Jules. Wake up," he said as he squeezed her fingers.

Nothing.

Meanwhile, Carl refused to be ignored. He came around the bed to look steadily at Mark. "You're sure you feel okay?"

Mark glared at the Max, but didn't comment beyond that. He'd already answered these questions. He was better than ever before. The reasons were complicated. First off, his time with his grizzly asleep had given him a new appreciation of exactly what his bear did for him. The creature gave the human focus and a grounding he'd never appreciated before. Second, the grizzly had his mate now, if she ever woke up. The bond between him and Julie was set in granite. Whether that was chemical or magic or simple luck, he didn't know, but it steadied him in ways he couldn't even express. He'd thought they were connected before, but this was deeper, more permanent and way more profound than he'd ever imagined was possible.

The two of them were joined at the soul. But that didn't make a damn bit of difference if Julie never woke up. He'd been ready to give up his life to save hers. The fact that it might have worked out the other way was killing him.

"She's my mate. I can't live without her."

Carl blew out a breath. Fortunately, he knew better than to argue. Grizzlies mated for life, and when one died, there was a fifty-fifty chance the other would go as well. Mark already knew which side of that equation he would go on merely because the thought of life without her was squeezing his chest to the point that he couldn't breathe.

"One step at a time," Carl said.

Mark didn't speak. He just watched Julie's chest and measured the steady rise and fall, aching for a change. A hitch. A deeper movement. Something that would indicate that she was coming back to him.

"Evil Einstein is talking," Carl said. "He's cut a deal with the DA in return for explanations about his research. His real name is Morris Holland and he's a grade-A nutjob from the Upper Peninsula. Parents were cross-species shifters. A wolf and a bear. God knows how that happened and nobody noticed, but he's apparently dedicated his life to activating his shifter DNA."

Mark shook his head. It was a well-known fact that cross-species parents produced non-shifting children. The idea that this Morris had somehow managed to activate latent DNA was both a miracle and a tragedy of psychotic proportions. Just what did he think would happen if he took his own drug? He'd become some bizarre mix of wolf and bear that would look like...

Oh, hell.

"The freaks who attacked Julie's cabin."

Carl nodded. "They were all of mixed heritage that had been activated."

"So shoot him up with his own shit and let him study what it feels like. And don't kill him until he's too weak to scream anymore."

"I've considered it."

Mark nodded. Fucker ought to die in his own science experiment. But logic told him that if something went south with Julie, they'd need Evil Einstein alive and competent. "How's Alan?"

Carl's voice was even as he spoke, but Mark understood the bite of tension beneath the words. "His fever's down. Vitals are stabilized. He's been in and out of consciousness, but the docs are keeping him quiet. His bear DNA has been switched on somehow, but it's beating the shit out of his body."

"So...better?"

Carl nodded, stark relief on his face. "Yeah. Better. And getting stronger every day."

"Good." Now if only Julie would wake, too, Mark might believe they were getting out of this disaster.

He looked down at her, his eyes narrowing. Had there been a shift in her breathing? Had her eyes twitched? With Carl distracting him, he couldn't watch her with his regular focus.

"You need to get some real sleep," Carl said. "In a bed."

"I just need some—"

"Coffee."

Mark and Carl froze at the rasping voice. Had that been Julie? He almost couldn't bring himself to believe. But he hadn't said it. And from Carl's face, it hadn't been the alpha, either.

Mark lifted her hand to his lips and squeezed her fingers. "I promise to get you a triple mocha if you'll just open your eyes. Come on, Jules. Extra whip with a drizzle of caramel." After hitting research mode with her a few days back, he knew exactly how she liked her caffeine and sugar.

Her eyelids fluttered, and she frowned. Carl moved to the side table and brought her a glass of water, pressing the straw against her lips. Young shifters were always dehydrated when they woke. Mark's bear dug at him, reminding him that no other man should serve his mate. It was true, but Mark was too busy gently chafing Julie's hand to handle the water.

"Come on, baby. Open those pretty brown eyes for me."

She didn't. But she did open her mouth enough for Carl to put the straw inside. And then she drank. She really drank the water, which was the best sign of approaching consciousness that he'd had from her. But the very next was even better.

She spit out the straw. "You promised me a mocha latte."

Then she opened her eyes. Relief flooded his system when their gazes connected. He could see everything in them. Groggy recognition and signs of temper. Every shifter on the planet came out of their first change with the exact same cranky pants attitude. Not to mention a killer hangover. But they could deal with that as long as she was awake. As long as she was alive.

Then her eyes slipped closed again.

"Wake up, baby," he said. "I've got news." If coffee couldn't lure her into awareness, then information would. He was sure of it.

And just like magic, her expression tightened into a frown. "I turned into a bear."

She'd turned partly into a bear. She hadn't the DNA for a full shift, but it had been enough for his grizzly to recognize her. For his bear to claim her and the mating bond to lock into place. But he would explain those details later. Right now, she had to accept that she was part shifter.

"Yes, you did," he said, keeping his voice carefully neutral. Not everyone wanted to be burdened with a strong animal side. For many, the costs far outweighed the benefits. If she hated what she'd become—

"Cool."

"What? Are you hot? Do you need—"

She opened her eyes to glare at him. "No, silly. It was cool. Will I be able to do it again?"

Now there was Julie, aware and demanding answers. He'd never seen a more beautiful sight. "Don't know. How about you get stronger and we'll try it again?"

"Maybe," Carl interrupted. "If you feel up to it. But don't push it and don't go trying anything without talking to us first."

Julie rolled her eyes. "Mother Hen," she drawled, making Mark laugh. Carl, too, though he tried to hide it.

"I'm your alpha now, Julie. You're going to have to listen to me."

Her eyes focused on him. "No one else does. Why do I have to?"

Carl growled at her, a sound that was half affection and half exasperation. "Mark is so *not* doing your orientation. He's a bad influence. And everyone does listen—"

"How's Alan?" she interrupted, the concern in her voice effectively deflating Carl's annoyance.

"Better. Stronger. And alive, thanks to you."

She shook her head. "I couldn't bond with him. I don't think he wanted it."

"But you kept him together until we could get there. I can't thank you enough for that."

She exhaled slowly, her eyes drifting shut. "I feel like I've been hit by a truck." She cracked an eye to stare at Mark. "Or a really big grizzly."

He smiled, leaning forward until he was within kissing distance. "Is that a bad thing?" He didn't want her to know how desperately he wanted to hear her answer. Apparently, she was okay with being a bear. Was she okay with him? Was she—

"You promised me news, and I'm not kissing you until I get it."

Well, okay. That was a promising start. At least she wasn't tossing him out of the room.

"You're a Gladwin shifter now. Alan's healing. Mad Einstein is in custody and helping, though most of us want to kill him slowly and painfully."

"Sign me up on that side."

He smiled. He liked her bloodthirsty side. But that meant he would wait to tell her that the cougar bitch had gotten away. Meanwhile, she shifted her legs without opening her eyes. Her body was waking, and she would likely get more irritable as the day went on. It took time to adjust to the steady presence of an animal side. But a couple analgesics or a few stiff shots would take care of that, too. Which meant now was the best time to give her the rest.

"I want to marry you, Julie. However you want, as soon as you want. We're bonded now, and I don't think I can live without you, but that's not why I want to marry you. I love you. Completely. Totally. I have since we were sixteen. My bear knew from the moment we kissed way back then, and again when you woke me from a sound sleep a week ago. But the man in me loves the way your mind works with such focus even when the rest of the world is going to hell. I love the way you laugh and that you give yourself so easily to everything you do. I love that you see through my bullshit and make me want you even when you're telling me

I'm an ass. Julie, every part of me loves you completely, totally, irrationally, and wonderfully. Please, for the love of God, will you say something?"

She stared at him, her eyes wide open and her mouth slightly ajar. She tried to push herself upright, but the bed blanket wasn't cooperating. It caught under her elbow as she shoved herself up. He wanted to help her—reached for her—but he held her other hand captive in his.

Carl pushed the correct button on the hospital bed, electronically sitting her upright. Not so fortunately, the alpha didn't have a muzzle on.

"Jesus, man, you have got to work on your timing."

Mark shot him a glare, but Julie pointed at the alpha. "What he said."

Oh. Right. Well, that sucked. Meanwhile, Julie spent a moment running her free hand through her hair to smooth it down. Mark caught her fingers and pulled them down to press another kiss to her knuckles.

"You have never looked more beautiful to me. And I know my timing sucks, but I wasn't going to let another second go by without telling you how much I love you. I do. I love you. Please say you feel something of the same for me."

She straightened up. "I did. Don't you remember? Well, maybe not because you were a bear at the time."

"I remember." Though in honesty, the meaning was fuzzy in his mind. He mostly remembered her tone and the way her scent had called to him. "But tell me again. Please?"

She took a deep breath. "I love you, Mark. I can't wait to

marry you. And as soon as I'm out of this hospital bed, I want to show you exactly how much." Then she gave him an impish look. "Um...does being a shifter mean that I'm constantly horny?"

His eyes widened. "Um, not usually."

"Huh. Okay. Then that must be because of you."

It took him a moment to understand what she was saying. And then her impish look turned downright sultry and nothing could keep him away. He crushed her to him, his mouth finding hers in a desperate rush of need. She met him with ease, her mouth open and receptive, but once he rushed in, the fireworks really began. She kissed him like he'd always dreamed. With passion. With need. With an underlying knowledge in the bond between them that he was hers and she was his. Mates. For life.

A nurse separated them. A harridan in white who physically dragged him back. "Mr. Robertson! Control yourself."

He was a half breath away from pushing her aside, but Cail held up his hand. "Sorry. She just agreed to marry him. He might have gotten a little too enthusiastic."

"No, he didn't," Julie said, as she pushed the woman away. "He was exactly as enthusiastic as—"

"Oh my God!" a woman exclaimed. "You're awake!"

Only one woman could make Mark table his lust. Julie's mother rushed in and maneuvered herself in front of Mark so she could hug her daughter. Mark stepped back then as Professor Simon entered as well, moving more slowly but with no less desire.

It was family, he realized. Her family, but now his as well. They would be part of his life forever, and, oddly enough, that felt really good.

"You're going to have to come out of your basement cave, you know," Carl said, sounding irritatingly pleased by the statement. "You can't isolate yourself in that pit any longer. She won't tolerate it, and it would be cruel to keep her from the world."

"I know," he said, startled to realize he was fine with it. "I can't wait."

And then Julie called his name, easily pulling him into the circle of her parents and sister, who was just joining them.

"Hey, everyone," she said. "I'd like to introduce you to my fiancé." Then she looked up at him. "We're going to live a very long and very happy life together."

What could he say to that except, "Yup."

Epilogue

Alan dragged his eyes open to a room flooded with sunlight. He'd always like the light, but this time he flinched away from it. And then suddenly, she was there.

Tonya.

Her face was drawn with worry, her hands tight where they gripped his arm.

"What's wrong?" he rasped.

She blinked twice before speaking, her voice heavy with irony. "Nothing's wrong except you've been running a temperature higher than a volcano for nearly a week."

Huh. Is that why he felt like an overbaked biscuit? God, even his skin seemed to crackle when he moved. Thankfully, she brought him water, and he drank the cup greedily. Flashes of memory returned to him. He'd been abducted right in the courthouse parking lot. Then that damned cage and all the who-knew-what that had been shoved into his arm.

Evil Einstein and that cougar bitch. She had been the worst. Einstein had just looked at him like a science project, but that bitch had sat and stared at him. Hours upon hours just like a fucking cat, and she hadn't said a word. At least not English words. There's been weird chants and strange potions shoved down his throat. And all the while, he'd felt the caress of her like slime on his skin.

And then…

Oh, hell. "Did I shift?"

Tonya's gaze slanted away. "Sort of."

He looked at her face, seeing the stark fear that she tried to hide. And then he remembered the rest. The prickly agony of fur spiking out of his skin. Not in a regular way, but in patches. The horror of a nose and mouth elongated and teeth that were sharp and irregular inside his mouth. And the fever. He remembered the fever sapping his strength and the bitch hissing in his ear when he was too weak to move.

And he remembered how much he hated her.

"So I'm a freak now," he said as he looked at his arms before him. Same bones, but the skin was patchy with dark spots. Same hands except the knuckles were larger, the fingers blunter.

"No!" Tonya said, gratifyingly vehement.

"It's okay. I was one already, though in a different way."

She turned to look at him, her blue eyes laser bright. "What do you mean?"

He meant a lot of things, none of which he could process or explain right now. "How'd you find me?"

"Mark turned on your phone. Used the GPS."

Right. Good idea. But... "Why'd it take a week?"

Silence.

He looked at Tonya and a familiar ache settled into his chest. Good God. He'd been gone for a week, trapped in that cage while Einstein experimented on him. He'd missed two court dates and at least one Gladwin pack meeting. And in all that time... "You guys didn't even realize I was missing."

She swallowed. "Carl got a text saying you had met someone. That you'd be gone for a while."

"Because I'm so irresponsible that I disappear for a week without finding a replacement, without emailing everyone at least twice. Without—" His voice choked off. He'd been covering the Gladwin paperwork almost since he could read. His father was never happier than when Alan announced the intention of becoming a lawyer. The Gladwins needed a lawyer in the family because good ones cost too damned much.

So he'd gone. He'd studied. And he'd become his brother's right-hand man for everything that the shifters were too twitchy to deal with. Paperwork. Court filings. Hell, he even did the taxes. All the details of living in this modern age were handled by Alan.

And no one had fucking realized he'd been missing.

"I'm sorry. We're all really sorry," she said.

Yeah. He got that. Except sorry wasn't cutting it with him right now. Fury itched right beneath his skin. A red haze of hatred rose up from his gut to choke off his words. Tonya was saying she was sorry. Tonya, the woman he'd loved since he was ten, was apologizing for not noticing him.

Like that was fucking unusual.

"Get out," he said. Except it didn't come out in cold, clipped tones. It wasn't his precise, businesslike way. No, the words were snarled. The meaning was ripped from his heart and thrown at her face.

"Alan—"

"Get. The. Fuck. Out."

Carl would have blustered at him. Becca would probably pat his hand and offer to get him some pie. Tonya, however, was a straight line in his mind. No bullshit, no fudging. She'd screwed up. They'd all screwed up, but she took the brunt of his rage because she was here.

"If you ever want to talk, just call me," she said as she straightened up. "Day or night."

He glared at her. "Not going to happen."

She dipped her chin, and her short honey-blond hair brushed over her eyes. He didn't know if it was an apology, an acknowledgment, or if she just had that much trouble looking at the freak he'd become. Whatever it was didn't matter. She stepped out of the room a moment later and was gone.

Six hours later, he was wide awake in his bed. It was night, the floor was quiet, and the nurses gossiped in low tones down the hall. Thanks to Becca he had a change of clothes. Thanks to Carl's visit an hour after Tonya, he had a good idea of just how bad everyone felt for not realizing he'd been abducted.

Somehow that didn't mean jack shit to him.

Now it was night, and he was dressed.

He snuck out of his room and slipped down the stairs. Ten

minutes later, he was hotwiring a motorcycle. He'd never stolen so much as a kiss from anyone, but he was taking this Harley after figuring out how to jack it from a video on the Internet.

Then he roared away, relishing the throb between his thighs and nursing the hatred in his soul. He couldn't deal with the Gladwin grizzlies. He refused to think about a single one of the ungrateful, self-absorbed bastards. Instead, he focused on the cat bitch. He was going to kill her. He was going to rip her heart from her chest then laugh as the light died from her eyes.

And he was going to do it alone.

His bear is in full pursuit.

See the next page for a preview of

FOR THE BEAR'S EYES ONLY

Available soon.

For the Bear's Eyes Only
By Kathy Lyons

*P*retty.

Alan Carman looked up in shock at the colors of the stars. It was a dark night without moon or clouds, which left him a clear view of the heavens. Red. Blue. Yellow. Pinpricks of light with Christmas-like halos. As if the stars were a very far away holiday display.

He blinked, doing his best to focus his thoughts. It was getting harder, especially with his fever coming back. It had been a week since leaving the hospital and whatever focus he'd had was now slipping away. Colors distracted him. Scents overpowered him. And he enjoyed the brute force use of his muscles like a Neanderthal. He'd always been a man who valued thinking. He ferreted out the reasons behind the actions and quietly sneered at people who couldn't use logic.

Now he was one of the dumb ones. Distracted by trivialities. Happy in raw strength. And unable to remember anything beyond this moment in time.

Good thing he was dying. He didn't know how long he could hold on to his mission. Too much distracted him and his thoughts splintered into fragments. He remembered a command.

Look at your hands.

Something about his hands was important.

So he focused downward to the flex of tendon and bone. He remembered typing elegant phrases on a computer. Even before that, he'd played with calligraphy as a boy. Beautiful strokes of ink on parchment. But when he looked down now, he didn't see long fingers with neatly trimmed nails. He saw hairy fists, knobby knuckles, pinprick claws.

A monster.

He was a monster now, and he hated pretty.

He had to keep it together for his mission. One last thing to do before he died. Kill the bitch who'd done this to him. Kill her for making him despise pretty. Kill her for destroying a good man. And he'd been a good man, he was sure, but he wasn't anymore.

Refocused on his purpose, he looked out at the parking lot. He studied the rusted trucks and mentally dissected the stench of piss and vomit. His attention slid to minute sensations as he leaned against the brick wall of a topless bar. He was deafened by the music and nauseated by the slime on the brick where it slicked his skin. And yet, unwilling, his gaze inevitably rose to the stars.

Pretty.

Then he winced as the already loud music exploded into the air. Someone was leaving the bar. Next came a man's voice, thick with liquor. A moment later, Alan saw his target draped around a tired-looking woman.

"Come on, honey," the bastard said. "It's a pretty night. We can see the stars."

"Nah, Johnny. I don't like the stars. I like what you got right here." She giggled, clearly drunk. But when Alan sniffed the air, working to isolate smells and their origin, he wasn't so sure. The man's scent was thick with alcohol, but hers wasn't so ugly. Then he watched her lift Johnny's wallet. Clever fingers, moving quickly as the two people wove their way to the back of the parking lot.

Good.

Alan kept himself in check while she pocketed all Johnny's cash then went for his watch. Might as well let her get what she needed. He counted the seconds, forcing himself to get to twenty before he struck. Long enough for the couple to stumble into the shadows with him.

Now.

Easy-peasy to reach out and grab the bastard by the throat. Monsters had quick reflexes and could crush a man's larynx with a single squeeze.

He didn't do it though it was disturbingly hard to control the impulse. Johnny was a drunk, a cheat, and a miserably bad father, but he didn't deserve death. So Alan held himself back. Besides, Alan needed the idiot alive. So he used his strength to pin the moron against a truck. And he didn't crush the larynx, though he did push it a little.

Fortunately, Johnny was sober enough to understand the

threat. His eyes bugged out and his fists froze at his side.

"Woah, mister," the woman began.

"Go back inside," Alan ordered. His voice was as rusty as the truck, but he forced the words out. "Johnny and I. Chat."

Once he'd been known for his delicate phrasing and precise word choice. But the monster was so close to the surface now, he had no complexity in his language.

"Call the—" Johnny tried, but Alan leaned in. No more oxygen for Johnny.

"Call the cops," Alan said. "I'll tell them about your hip pocket." It's where she'd stashed Johnny's watch.

The side of her mouth tilted up in a smirk. "Like anybody cares."

True. He knew cops, and they didn't much care about petty theft. Not when it was someone like Johnny getting picked. Time for a different tack. With his free hand, he pulled a couple twenties out of his front pocket. He'd planned to use it for dinner, but after smelling Johnny up close, he'd lost his appetite. "Take this. We're gonna talk. About his wife. Kids."

She took the bills quickly but kept her tone hard. "If he ends up dead, I know what you look like."

No, she didn't. Not the real him. But he didn't argue. "Okay."

"Okay." She turned and sauntered back to the bar while Johnny sputtered in disgust.

Alan took a moment. It was a habit he'd developed as a man to organize his thoughts. But with the monster so strong, all he could do was think about Johnny's emotions as they marched across his face. Anger. Frustration. A slow relaxation of fear. That last one was a problem. He needed Johnny pissing-his-pants ter-rified. So he punched the man in his thick gut.

Johnny doubled over from the pain. Alan let him gag, but then straightened him back up. Except now he could see the bastard's eyes. Cougar slits, glowing a dull lime green. The man was try-ing to shift, but Alan knew it was too soon. The idiot had been a cougar just hours ago. No way was he capable of changing again this fast.

"Nice try," Alan said as he increased pressure on Johnny's throat. "How do you think I found you? I tracked cougar piss. Followed you here."

The bastard frowned, and Alan watched his nose twitch as he tried to sort out Alan's species by scent. Good luck with that. There was no species like him. But he did like seeing the terror of people's faces when they figured that out. So he let Johnny sniff. And just to make sure it was clear, he relaxed into the horror of his own body. It was as simple as breathing and he could do it anytime he wanted, probably because he was a monster first, and a man a distant second. He let the patchy fur rise, bringing its own stench with it. His joints ached and his muscles thickened. His sharp nails became pronounced claws and, worst of all, his nose and mouth stretched around sharp teeth. Even if Johnny couldn't see clearly what was happening, the *wrongness* of Alan's cells became clear to anyone with a shifter nose.

And that's when Johnny really began to sweat. "What are you?" he gagged. "Bear?"

"Monster. Looking for Elisabeth Oltheten."

"She ain't part of us no more. We kicked her outta the pride."

Lions had prides, not cougars. But maybe the cougar shifter knew best. Part of Alan wondered, but the rest of him didn't care.

"I need to find Elisabeth Oltheten," he said.

"I don't know where she is!"

"She's one of you—"

"She started the war with the wolves. The one that got all of us kilt!" Johnny was spitting now. The wet added its own reek to the encounter, and Alan wanted nothing more than to leave.

"Killed, you idiot. Not kilt."

"Wot?"

Not the brightest bulb and drunk as well. Alan focused on the basics: slowly choking Johnny until he had the man's full attention.

"Where's Elisabeth Oltheten?" he repeated.

"I don't know!"

"Find out."

"How? We got no one left!"

Not true. He knew that because he'd been carefully stalking the cougars for a week now.

"You didn't die, Johnny. Your brother didn't die. You got four people left in your clan, plus your kids. Someone has to know—"

"We don't know shit!"

Truer words were never spoken, but Alan didn't have the luxury of finding better sources. "Find out or I'm going to do to your kids what she did to me." He leaned in, making sure Johnny saw his sharp teeth in a bearlike jaw. "Take a good whiff."

The man choked on his fear, spitting out his terrified words. "Don't you touch my boy!"

The bastard had one son and two daughters, but clearly he didn't give a shit about the girls. Which was really stupid because among cat shifters, it was the females who had the brains.

"Find Elisabeth." He pulled a card out of his pocket. All it had was a single email address on it and a logo of an ogre. A little obvious, style wise, but it was meant for male cats with limited intelligence. He slid it into Johnny's shirt pocket. "You find something and email."

Johnny blinked, his eyes watering either from terror or the stench. "That's it? Anything? I just email you?"

"It better be true. Or I'll hurt your boy."

Alan waited a moment longer, letting the threat sink in. Then after a last shove against the bastard's neck, he spun around and loped off into the dark.

About the Author

Kathy Lyons is the wild, adventurous half of *USA Today* bestselling author Jade Lee. A lover of all things fantastical, Kathy spent much of her childhood in Narnia, Middle Earth, Amber, and Earthsea, just to name a few. There is nothing she adores more than turning an ordinary day into something magical, which is what happens all the time in her books. Winner of several industry awards, including the Prism Best of the Best Award, a Romantic Times Reviewers' Choice Award, and Fresh Fiction's Steamiest Read, Kathy has published more than fifty romance novels, and she's just getting started.

Check out her latest news at:

KathyLyons.com

Facebook.com/JadeLeeBooks

Twitter: @JadeLeeAuthor

CPSIA information can be obtained at www.ICGtesting.com
Printed in the USA
LVOW11s0417210916

505493LV00001B/15/P